THE SMALL DARK ROOM OF THE SOUL
AND OTHER STORIES

TO TRINKA,

IT WAS GREAT
MEETING YOU. I HOPE I
HAD 1/10000 TH THE RATTLING
OF YOUR BRAIN CELLS THAT
OWSLEY DID. HIS
HOBBIES HAD A BIG
INFLUENCE ON MINE. I
THINK YOU'LL SEE IT HERE.

MATT

The Small Dark Room of the Soul

AND OTHER STORIES

Matthew J. Pallamary

San Diego Writers' Monthly

Published by
San Diego Writers' Monthly
3910 Chapman Street
San Diego, CA 92110

Library of Congress Cataloging in Publication Data
Library of Congress Number 94-067377

Pallamary, Matthew, J.

  The Small Dark Room Of The Soul And Other Stories
    p. cm.

  ISBN 1-885516-00-2

Cover illustration: Derek Hodges & Sandra Welch

Dedication & Acknowledgments

First, foremost, and utmost the author would like to express his deepest and sincere appreciation for the loving, nurturing guidance, and discipline received from his illegitimate mother, Joan Oppenheimer, and his legitimate mother Colleen Kennedy. Words don't make it here.

I would also like to thank: Mike MacCarthy, Sandra Welch, and Derek Hodges for their hard work and dedication to this project; the members of Joan Oppenheimer's writing workshops — particularly Eric Hart for his enthusiasm; Terry, Sue, and Eric Bruns; Chris LaBosky, June DiStefano and Eric Hart again for proofing; Nancy Holder and the members of the "Holder In The Wall Gang" wherever they may be; Lynn Ford for picking me up when I was crawling; Barnaby and Mary Conrad, Paul Lazarus, Sid Stebel and everyone else involved with The Santa Barbara Writer's Conference; Jean Jenkins and the staff of The Southern California Writer's Conference * S D; Saddleback Writer's Conference; The wonderful gang at *San Diego Writers' Monthly*; and Judy Reeves and Ray Bruce at The Writing Center in San Diego for all their encouragement and support.

Last, but not least, I'd like to thank Lidia for riding with me on this roller coaster and everyone else (you know who you are) for giving me your enthusiasm when mine was lagging.

Matt

February 13, 1994

INTRODUCTION

There can be no light without darkness.

The sun cannot rise without the night preceding it, and the setting sun of the day must inevitably fade to black. If life were all sunshine and roses, there would be no contrast. Perpetual sunshine would be both blinding and devastating. We need the darkness. It is an integral part of the whole.

Part of us.

Horror stories are a reflection of our darker side. In an age of very real terrors like A.I.D.S., cancer, and terrorism, stories that frighten us can perform a useful function by allowing readers to live out and experience fear in a controlled fashion and deal with horror on their own terms. If it gets to be too much, they can always close the book and put it away. Experiencing horror in this way works as an anxiety release because it is a tangible way to deal with and escape the terrors of modern living.

The emotion of horror keeps us in touch with the darker aspects of ourselves while allowing us to confront our own vulnerability and inevitable death. Reading horror is a valve that allows steam to escape when the buildup is too great, yet the fictionality of it gives us an escape from a confrontation that could overwhelm us. It provides a cathartic release without oppressing us with more than we can handle.

Too often we shun our dark side in hopes that if we don't see it, it doesn't exist. Yet give us an Ed Gein, Charlie Manson,

Ted Bundy, Hannibal Lecter, Jeffrey Dahmer, or any other grisly example of the dark side of human nature, and we express a morbid fascination that borders on frenzy.

We can't help but slow down on the highway to gawk at the carnage of another's untimely, messy death or sneak that guilty peek at another's deformity or misfortune.

We just have to look.

How many Jeffrey Dahmer jokes have we laughed at, then in the same breath said how disgusting it all is.

Strange creatures, human beings.

Fact is, our dark side is an inescapable part of our makeup. There's a little bit of Hannibal and Jeffrey in all of us, the problem is most of us don't want to acknowledge it.

Through the ages, countless spiritual disciplines have urged us to look within ourselves and seek the truth. Part of that truth resides in a small, dark room — one we are afraid to enter. If we can only push aside the dark door of fear that holds us at bay and rescue the part of our souls that cringes in the dark, we might come to a better understanding of what makes us tick.

We have to take this unmentionable part of ourselves out into the light of truth so we can know its nature, because if we are to confront the uncomfortable truth, we must look in the face of the demon and admit that it is in us. When we're finished, we can let the monster crawl back into its dark abyss until the next play time.

If you're timid of spirit and afraid of the dark, it's time to take a look at what lies behind your own door of fear so you can glimpse the twisted evil that lies in *all* of us. Within these pages we can play with it, poke at it, and probe it in hopes that we may better understand the wholeness that makes up our being.

Who says we can't have fun doing it? After all, the little monster *is* part of us.

March 1994   *M. P.*

TABLE OF CONTENTS

MOON DANCE

Collete slid the tight black leather miniskirt up over her hips. Frank's favorite; the one he always insisted she wear. She zippered it and buttoned her blouse, leaving the top two buttons open, exposing her cleavage. Turning from side to side, she ran her hands down her thighs and studied her slim profile in the mirror. At least on this occasion black was appropriate. With a tight smile, she touched up her blush, then checked her eye shadow and shook her dark hair back.

Frank, my darling, you'd love to get your hands on this little package, wouldn't you?

She put on her heels, dabbed Tatiana behind her ears, then trailed a perfumed finger between her breasts — something else Frank insisted on. And why not? This was their anniversary, wasn't it?.

Grabbing her purse and keys, she stepped out into the night and looked up at the full moon. Frank had a thing for full moons. Said it brought out the animal in him — and boy had it ever. She glanced at the scar on the back of her hand as she slid the key into the car door, then hopped in, anxious to be on time for her date. Frank insisted on promptness.

She backed out of the driveway and drove past the storybook

houses lining her street. As she drove, she remembered the first time she saw Frank. Blond hair, bright blue eyes and flawless white teeth. Irresistible. As if his handsome features weren't enough, he had sexy shoulders, nice pecs and a washboard stomach. The care he took of himself and his possessions bordered on fastidiousness. Like the houses on her street, with Frank, everything had to be perfect, especially his fire-engine red Porsche. His baby.

Frank had it all. Good looks, money and charm. Attentive and protective, he exuded strength and maturity. When he walked into a room, all eyes went to him. Everyone said what a wonderful catch he'd be for some lucky girl. Colette had been the lucky one. She smiled to herself. The girls at work had all been jealous.

She pulled onto the freeway and eased the car up to seventy. She could hardly believe the way Frank courted her. Expensive wine, fancy restaurants and candlelit dinners. Romantic as hell and everything just right. She couldn't wait for him to pop the question.

Colette drove a few miles north, took her exit and worked her way through the side streets. Their wedding had been right out of a romance novel. Frank looked dashing and handsome in his tux and Colette felt like a princess in her white lace gown. Together they shared a magical day of gifts, warm wishes and happiness. She saw it in her mother's eyes. "You're so lucky, honey."

She found the street, pulled through the wrought iron gates and drove slowly through the manicured grounds, admiring the flowers and landscaping, wondering what lay below the surface.

No sooner had their marriage been consummated, when he changed and his true self came to the surface. Everything had to be perfect for him, including herself.

She pulled to the side, killed the engine and climbed out into the moonlight. She tried so hard to please him, but if things weren't right — she caught herself. It wasn't going to happen. Not tonight. Not ever again. She studied the cuts and burns on her arms, shuddering at the memory of the beatings. Frank's hands had been on her once too often.

She looked up at the manicured grave. Its granite stone glistened in the moonlight, perfect and polished, just like Frank.

Then she slipped off her shoes, stepped onto the grave, and danced.

HIGH ALTITUDE COOKING

The September morning sky hung thick with leaden clouds when Larry Cook set out at the trail head. A northern breeze whisked through the pines, chilling him with a soft chorus of whispers. He looked up at the towering mountain faces. Snow-dusted summits and craggy rock outcroppings surrounded him.

Onward and upward. He took a deep breath and snugged the straps on his pack, then set out, intent on making his way to the high country.

A short way up the trail, he stopped to wipe his brow and catch his breath. The sixty-pound pack and thin air made the climb harder than he'd anticipated, but he was determined not to turn back.

I can't believe it. This week I'm here. Last week I'm sitting at Ken's bar. "Bet you five hundred bones, you can't make it to the top," Ken said, refilling Larry's mug.

"You're on, sucker." Larry pushed his hair back from his forehead, then rubbed his beer belly. "Even though I don't have any experience in the woods, I'm in great shape. For five hundred I'll be ready for anything."

"Put your money where your mouth is." Ken slapped five

one hundred dollar bills on the bar. "My uncle runs his own store. Yukon Jack's. You can rent your gear there. Talk to him. He's an expert in high altitude cooking and survival techniques. Got trapped in the mountains with a group back in the Fifties. He was the only one who survived."

"How'd he do it?"

Ken smiled. "Never talked about it much."

"But he still backpacks."

"He says once you get a taste for it ...."

"Bullshit! I could probably teach your uncle a few things. I'll learn as I go. On my own."

Shooting fish in a barrel. He looked up the trail. "I can do this," he said between breaths. "I'm a goddamned Grizzly Adams."

He set off again climbing, then resting, then climbing, slowly working his way up the trail. By late morning he'd made it past a rock-strewn gully and pushed his way into the pine and birch that covered the lower slopes. He stopped for lunch at a fork in the trail, pulled out his map and compass, and checked his progress. *About two miles in.* He studied the contours of his map, tracing with his finger. *Climbed about two thousand feet.*

He could still hear the gravelly voice of Ken's uncle. "You sure you're up to this, son?" The old man stroked his salt and pepper beard and appraised Larry, then the phone rang. He held up a finger. "Back in a minute."

Larry glanced around to be sure no one was looking and slipped a hundred twenty dollar survival knife under his jacket. The old man came back a few minutes later with a map. His eyes narrowed. For a moment Larry thought he'd been caught, then the old man's eyes brightened. "The El Diablo Loco trail.

Right here." He put his finger on the map. "Up near the Big Pine section of the Sierra Nevadas. Nothing up there but bears, birds and squirrels." He clapped his bony hand on Larry's shoulder. "You're gonna love it."

I am loving it. Larry propped his feet up on his pack and put his hands behind his head. *Tough going. But this is great. No one around.* He felt his eyes getting heavy.

Two squirrels ran across the branches above him and scampered down the trunk of the tree next to where he sat. He lifted his head and they stopped. One of them sat up on its haunches and studied Larry a moment before chattering its disapproval, then it bounded off into the surrounding foliage.

Cute little bastards. He smiled to himself and dozed off.

He sat up, jolted from his nap. More chattering. He listened attentively. There it was again.

Those squirrels sure are pissed. He cocked his head and cupped his hand behind his ear. *Weird. That ain't squirrels. It's — people!*

"Howard," a whiney voice said from down the trail. "I told you we shouldn't have come. This isn't good for your heart."

"Wrong, Mildred," the gravelly voice replied. "*You* shouldn't have come. If anything's bad for my heart, it's your constant nagging."

No, can't be...

"How could you say such a thing — after all these years?"

"Too many years."

I'm getting out of here before they see me. I'm not gonna put up with all that jabbering. Larry stood, shouldered his pack and turned to head up the trail, but the whiney voice stopped him before he could escape.

"Young man."

Larry's shoulders tightened. *Busted.*

He turned and scowled at the approaching couple. Ken's uncle and some old bat.

"Young man," the woman repeated. "Could you talk to my husband and tell him this is bad for his health?"

Larry studied her: stocky with streaked brown hair and a doughy face which held a frown that looked permanent. She appeared to be in her late fifties.

He nodded at the two of them. He hadn't seen her in Yukon Jack's. *The uncle's probably in on it with Ken. Wants to watch me fuck up.*

"Your husband's done this before." Larry studied the man's smoldering eyes. His defiant look and the lines on his face made him look older than his nagging wife. "He runs a damn backpacking store!"

"He's too frail for this strenuous activity."

I don't need this shit.

"Don't mind my wife," the old man said, winking. "She's a little overwrought, that's all."

"No shit, Sherlock. Sounds like you should have left her at home."

"Howard would be lost without me." The woman put a meaty hand on her husband's shoulder. "He needs me to take care of him."

"No one asked you to come." Something flickered in the old man's eyes.

A chill raced up Larry's spine. "Look, you nursing home rejects," he said. "Leave me out of your bullshit problems."

They both looked at him for a moment, their faces blank, then resumed their argument. Larry left.

They didn't notice.

The sky dimmed with the coming of sunset, but Larry couldn't see the sun. The thick carpet of clouds shrouding it hadn't changed since morning. The trail opened onto a large field, making it harder to follow. He did his best, but knew nightfall would approach quickly. He wanted to get out of the open.

When he got to the trees on the other side, he lost the trail. He went about a half mile into the woods in a futile effort to regain it but realized he was tired and hungry. The fading light made it hard to read his compass, so he found a small clearing and stopped. *I'll find the trail in the morning.*

He set up his propane stove and took out his mess kit. *Let's see what's on the menu.* He pulled out a package of freeze-dried beef stroganoff, mixed it with water and cooked it. *So this is what high altitude cooking is all about. Ain't shit. What the hell could that old geezer have shown me? How to light a match?* He chuckled at his own joke.

After eating, he unrolled his sleeping bag and stowed everything else in his pack. The cloud cover had disappeared, leaving a clear sky. He decided against pitching his tent and opted to sleep under the stars. Exhausted, he leaned his pack against a tree, crawled into his sleeping bag and fell asleep.

He awoke to a sound of tearing, accompanied by scratching and grunting noises. Rolling onto his side, he looked over at the tree. A few feet from his head, he saw a massive black form in the moonlight, pawing and shredding his pack with its teeth and claws.

Fucking bear! Larry's breath caught in his chest. He froze, afraid to move. *What's he gonna do? He's eating my food and wrecking my pack. What do I do?* He thought of yelling. *No, that'll piss him off. He'll come after me.*

Larry inched the sleeping bag up over his head and watched the bear through an opening in the top. Though the bag was warm, cold sweat poured off him. His teeth chattered and his heart hammered in his chest. He bit down hard on his lip and drew blood.

God, what if he smells my blood, my sweat?

He lay motionless as the bear ripped the pack apart and devoured his food.

A branch snapped somewhere behind him. Larry jumped. The bear turned toward him, reared up on its hind legs and moved its head from side to side before stopping, its eyes seemingly locked on Larry's. It lowered itself to its forepaws and lumbered toward the sleeping bag. Larry scrunched his eyes shut as the bear's snout came close to his head. A moment later the hot stench of the animal's breath filled his nostrils.

Our Father who art in Heaven...

A blast of hot breath exploded in his face as the bear barked. Larry lost control of his bladder. Wet warmth spread. He couldn't stop himself from shivering, then he sneezed.

The bear bounded off into the surrounding woods.

Larry opened one eye, then the other.

Gone.

He unclenched his teeth, wincing as he pulled them from his lip. They'd gone all the way through. A hot flush of blood filled his mouth and he blacked out.

Larry opened his eyes to morning light. The shroud had returned to the sky. His lip throbbed. Blood had crusted on his chin and neck. His body ached from the previous day's hike. Crawling out of his sleeping bag, he examined the remains of his pack. The frame hung broken and twisted like the aftermath of a train wreck. Shredded cloth and paper lay strewn about the base of the tree. His map had been destroyed, his compass shattered, its needle hopelessly mangled.

A gust of wind kicked up, bringing with it the first driving flakes of cold, biting snow. Larry shivered, half from cold, half from fear. All he had were the clothes on his back and his sleeping bag.

Who the hell says I'm not the outdoor type? This ain't shit. He stumbled off in search of the trail, back in the direction he thought the field might be. Snow fell thicker and heavier. Larry stepped up his pace.

Goddamned Grizzly Adams. That's what I am.

He wandered for a couple of hours before stopping and sitting against a tree to catch his breath. Snow covered the ground. He still hadn't found the clearing. Pulling the sleeping bag around his shoulders, he tried to orient himself, but the landscape had no recognizable features. Hunger gnawed at his gut and his throat felt dry. His lip throbbed. Scraping up a handful of snow, he filled his mouth, greedily swallowing the water as it melted. He leaned back, closed his eyes, and fell asleep.

When Larry awoke, fresh snow blanketed him and the surrounding terrain. He stood, shook off the white powder and stretched. The snow continued to fall.

Got to keep going — find the trail — find my way out of here. Wonder what happened to Ken's uncle and the old broad. Maybe they'll have food.

He felt weak but pushed on. The sky turned darker. *Night's coming — got to make a camp — build a fire. Only one book of matches — got to make them count.*

He found a spot in a semi-circle of jagged boulders to shelter himself from the wind and gathered wood. He cleared away some snow to build a fire, but his hands were numb and the wood wet. He went through most of his matches trying to get the fire lit, but it wouldn't catch. He decided to save his last two matches, climbed into his sleeping bag and huddled close to the rocks to wait out the night.

By daybreak the snow had stopped. The sun rose from behind a distant peak, but the cold air numbed him. He clapped his hands and stamped his feet to warm them, but it didn't help. He set off in hopes of finding the trail and restoring his circulation. As the sun gained altitude, the snow began to melt until he found himself sloshing through puddles. He tried to avoid them at first, but after his feet were soaked, he didn't care. That night he used his last two matches trying to light a fire, once more thwarted by wet wood. He spent the night sleeping fitfully, fighting pangs of hunger.

Larry met the new day with a fever, chills and aching joints. His throat felt sore and his lungs congested. Each cough crashed through his head like a battering ram. He climbed out of his sleeping bag and staggered through the woods, dragging it behind him, sometimes falling, sometimes sleeping where he fell. He drifted in and out of consciousness, imagining himself in warm places with food when he slept, then waking to harsh reality. He no longer knew what day it was, where he'd been, or where he was trying to go.

Finally, he stumbled over a rock and fell to the ground. He didn't have the strength or will power to get up again. He lay laughing at his ridiculous predicament until his pain was too much, then he cried and sought refuge in the darkness of unconsciousness.

God, I'm dreaming again. It smells so good. He opened his eyes. *I'm awake and alive — and the smell's still there. I'm so hungry I'm imagining this.*

It took all his will to stand and a superhuman effort to walk. A sweet smell wafted to his nostrils; the hope of finding its source the only thing that kept him conscious. He stopped and scanned the surrounding woods. A tiny orange flicker caught his eye. A rush of adrenaline surged through him.

My God. A fire.

He crashed through the underbrush, stumbling in the direction of the glow. Branches pulled at his hair and tore at his skin, but he didn't care. Two simple, primal thoughts drove him: *Food. Warmth.*

He stumbled into the campsite, crying for help.

No response.

Two packs stood against a tree and a large pot of stew simmered over the fire.

"Help, somebody, anybody! Is anyone here?" he croaked.

Silence.

He couldn't control himself. *Whoever it is, they'll understand.* He found a bowl by the fire, filled it with stew and ate, marveling at the huge chunks of stringy meat that filled the pot.

Must be bear stew. I've never tasted anything so incredible in all my life.

When he'd eaten half the bowl, his stomach knotted and he vomited. Calming himself, he ate again, slowly this time. *Just a few bites.* When he'd eaten all he thought he could hold without getting sick, he curled up in his sleeping bag and fell asleep, waiting for his savior.

He felt someone watching him.

No, please God, no. Not another bear.

He opened his eyes, blinking, and gazed into the lively brown eyes of a weathered, angular face. *Ken's uncle.* "You!" Larry gasped. "I - I'm sorry. I was...." He burst into tears.

"Calm down, son," the wiry old man said in his gravelly voice. The firelight danced in his eyes, reflecting amusement. "I understand." He stroked his speckled beard, stirred the stew and tasted it.

Calmed by the man's voice, Larry crawled out of his sleeping bag and sat upright in front of the fire. The old man ladled portions of stew into two bowls and handed one to Larry.

"I - I don't know how to thank you." Larry took the bowl in shaking hands. "You've saved my life. I've been lost for days." He stuffed a piece of stringy meat into his mouth, chewed, then swallowed. "This stew is wonderful."

The old man wiped his mouth with the back of his hand and talked as he chewed. "Can't take the credit for this. It's my wife. She makes great stew."

Larry looked over at the two packs leaning against the tree, then back to his host. A broad smile filled the old man's face.

Larry stopped chewing.

"Glad you came along when you did," the old man said. His eyes glittered as he pulled an axe out from behind a log, raised it and came at Larry. "I was just about out of food."

Larry hurled hot stew into his face. The old timer howled and staggered backward, arms flailing for balance. Larry drove his head into the old man's chest, trapping the axe between the two of them.

Crimson jetted from the old man's neck, spraying Larry's face with its hot stickiness. A gurgling sound came from deep in the old man's throat. Larry's tongue shot out, tasting rich saltiness. He stopped, horrified to see the old man twitching as life blood spewed onto the ground.

Such a waste.

Larry licked again. *The hell with the stew.* He sank his teeth into the open wound. *I like my meat fresh.*

"I told you...."

He recognized Ken's voice and froze.

"Once you get a taste for it...."

BLIND FAITH

Gifted. That's how they described Marie and the strange abilities that came to her as naturally as reading and writing came to others. She had inklings of them as a child but assumed that everyone else experienced the same things. She never thought of herself as different.

Through her formative years, she shrouded her private and unusual mental life, sharing it with no one. When she grew older, and the change occurred, Marie became bitter and entertained thoughts of suicide.

Her small circle of friends envied her heightened awareness, but she thought of it as a curse and would have traded it in an instant to regain the one perception that mysteriously sublimated when the rest of her senses blossomed. It seemed as if her senses became like a gang of unruly schoolchildren ostracizing one of their own in favor of a stranger.

Normally, her highly developed intuition was referred to as the sixth sense, but in Marie's case, she still had only five.

She remembered sight as a child, longed for it. The blue of the sky, brilliant crimson sunsets, lush green grass, and the reds, violets, and subtle shadings of flowers.

As her psychic abilities grew, darkness crept in like gradual layers of gauze: first in increasing shades of gray, then by the age of twenty-one, unrelieved black. Her moods followed suit.

With each layer blanketing her like wrap after wrap of gauze, came a corresponding increase in the acuteness of her other senses, especially the unseen one that gave her extrasensory perception. Doctors and psychiatrists had no answers. Her eyes appeared to function normally, yet Marie still lived in a world of darkness.

As a blind adult, she earned a modest income giving "readings," usually by getting impressions from an article of clothing or jewelry, but she could also feel the person's thoughts, sensing them as subtle vibrations. To do this she had to place her hands on their head.

When she did, she envisioned their thoughts in brief flashes like a camera shutter flipping open, burning the image into her mind like light on a photographic plate. These "snapshots" she committed to memory to study for the significant details they revealed. By talking to her subject, Marie received a collection of mental pictures that she sorted through to find the answers her clients sought.

Through the years, she'd seen a lot — often more than she wished, but for the most part only mundane things like the misplaced wedding band of the woman who sat across from her. She hated these sessions and resented her clients, but she needed the money.

"The last time I remember seeing it was two nights ago," the whining voice said.

Marie pictured an overweight middle-aged woman probably wringing her hands. The heavy smell of Lady Stetson filled the air, overpowering a faint scent of talcum powder. The odor of cigarettes and fish wafted from the woman's mouth each time she spoke. Marie wanted to gag.

"I took it off before I went to bed and thought I put it on the night stand, but when I woke up, it wasn't there."

"I can't promise I'll find it, Mrs. Mitchell." Marie held her hands out in front of her. "But if I can read your thoughts, maybe I can find out what happened to it." She motioned for the woman to come closer. "I need to place my hands on your head. Then I want you to talk through what you did."

She felt stiffened hair and smelled hair spray. "Go ahead," Marie said when her hands felt comfortable. "Tell me what you remember."

"I remember walking up the stairs and taking it off."

Marie's mind flashed on the image of the woman sliding the ring off her finger.

"Then the phone rang. I picked it up in the hall."

A white French phone on an antique table in a hall with textured wallpaper.

"It was my son calling about some of his school records."

A hand with a pen, the ring lying beside it.

"I heard a crash from downstairs, grabbed the ring and went down. The cat had knocked something off the counter."

A broken cookie jar on the floor. A ringless hand on the broom sweeping. The ring on the counter.

"When I finished cleaning, I went to bed. My husband was already asleep. When I woke up in the morning, he had already left for work. The ring wasn't in its usual spot. I looked everywhere."

The kitchen. Signs of a hasty breakfast. A newspaper on the counter where the ring had been. A headline, "Strangler Strikes." A tiny glint of gold behind the blender.

"Behind the blender," Marie blurted. "It was knocked there by the newspaper."

Marie felt the woman jump under her touch. She imagined the surprised expression, blinking eyes.

"I was so worried that I'd lost it."

An hour later the woman called, confirming Marie's findings.

When the doorbell rang the following morning, Marie sighed, anticipating only one more boring request from another overwrought crybaby wanting to find a misplaced wedding band or lost cat. When the ringing stopped, she sensed something different.

She felt her visitor's apprehension, which wasn't so unusual, but behind it she sensed an urgency that made the hairs on the back of her neck stand. This one had a real problem.

She rose from her chair and went toward the door, her own urgency rising with each step. The image of the newspaper headline flashed in her mind. "Strangler Strikes." Her heart thudded in her ears as her hand found the knob. A sudden excitement coursed through her. She savored the rare moment, then something spurred her on: an eagerness and curiosity to confront whatever troubled the person on the other side of the door.

She turned the knob and yanked it open until the door jerked on the security chain. "Who is it?" she said into the gap.

"Lieutenant Mitchell. San Diego Police. Homicide." The voice sounded tired, heavy. "Are you Marie Parsons?"

"How do you know my name? What do you want?"

"You spoke with my wife yesterday. Helped her find a ring."

"Mrs. Mitchell. Yes. Is she all right?"

"Couldn't be better. All she's talked about is how you found her ring. She's pleased with all you've done. She speaks very highly of you."

Marie felt her cheeks flush. "And what can I do for you, Lieutenant Mitchell?"

"Well — um — it's kind of — well. I don't quite know. May I come in?"

Marie hesitated. The impressions he gave her were sincere, but his tension worried her. "Excuse me for being suspicious, but may I see your badge?"

"I thought you were blind."

"I have a well developed sense of touch."

"Yes, of course. I should've known."

The rustle of clothing. The sound of a sleeve brushing against the door. She reached up and felt a large, warm hand, bony knuckles, then the touch of cold metal. She took the badge and ran her fingers over its surface.

She saw the image of a tall man with a crew-cut, sharp, jutting jaw and kind, but weary brown eyes. Satisfied, she handed the badge back and let him in.

"Please, sit down, Lieutenant Mitchell." She gestured toward a chair. "Tell me what's troubling you."

The sound of a large man settling into a chair.

"I don't have any right to ask you this. It goes against department policy, but frankly I'm stuck. You're the only one who might be able to help me."

"This is a police matter?"

"Yes."

A surge of excitement danced through her. She struggled to keep her composure as she lowered herself into the overstuffed chair across from Lieutenant Mitchell. "What is it you think I can help you with?"

"Do you listen to the news?"

"It's about the strangler, isn't it?"

A subdued gasp. "Amazing. How did you know?"

Marie allowed herself a smile.

"They're calling him the Door-To-Door Strangler. We think he's posing as a salesman, a milkman, a plumber, or some other delivery man or serviceman. He smooth-talks his way into his victims' houses and strangles them."

"Hasn't he been up in the Los Angeles area?"

"He may have moved down here. We've had a couple of murders that follow his pattern." He paused. "We think we have a·witness and a suspect."

Marie put her hand to her chest. "If you have a suspect and a witness, what do you need me for?"

"Our witness is a young girl, but she's in shock. Hasn't said a word. I was hoping you might be able to read her thoughts, give us a lead, maybe a description of the killer. See if it matches. I know it wouldn't hold up in court, but it might give us something to go on. We want to be as sure as we can that we don't have a copycat."

Marie thought of what it would be like to read the thoughts of a murder witness and shuddered. Her palms were sweaty. She wiped them on her dress. "I've — I've never done anything like that." Her throat felt dry.

She thought of the mundane things she had been seeing. A dullness crept over her, then she thought of the murder witness with a delicious tingle. Why not? She'd be under police protection. "All right." She nodded. "If you think it'll help."

The smell of cigarette smoke, the sounds of voices, ringing phones and clacking typewriters met Marie as she entered the police station on the strong arm of Lieutenant Mitchell. He made her feel safe and protected as he led her to a quieter part of the station.

Marie sensed two other people in the small room. Both sets of thoughts felt strained, emotional, but she had a stronger sense of the young girl's. Though wrapped in darkness and terror, their relative innocence revealed they were the thoughts of a child.

Instead of frightening her, the fear Marie sensed stimulated her. Without a word, she took a seat next to the child and placed her hands on her head. Soft, long hair. Tender skin. The smell of shampoo. Beneath it rigidness. Tension.

The first impression jolted her. She pulled her hands away as though she'd been shocked. When she put them back, the flashing images pressed her to her seat in a mixture of fear and exhilaration.

A view through a crack in a door. A young woman holding it open.

Another flash.

A tall, sandy-haired man with empty, darting eyes. Blue like a winter sky.

Flash.

The man looking around. Talking. Smiling. A young woman — Mommy — turning her back.

Flash.

The man reaching for her neck.

Flash.

A close-up of hands grabbing at Mommy's throat, her mouth wide in a strangled scream, eyes bulging, face a deep red.

Blackness.

A wave of dizziness swept through Marie as though someone had drugged her. She felt the sensation of spinning. Falling. Strong hands caught her.

When she regained consciousness, the first image that came to mind was a close-up of the hands closing on the woman's throat. A chill danced down her spine as though those very hands caressed her back.

She gave Mitchell a detailed description of the man and her mental photographs then had him take her home.

He called two days later.

"How are you feeling, Miss Parsons?"

"Fine thank you. It's nice of you to call."

"You gave me a little scare."

"I appreciate your concern."

"Aside from checking on you, I called to give you some good news and some not-so-good news."

Marie's breath caught in her throat. "Give me the good news first."

The good news is that we've formally pressed charges against our suspect."

The image of the hands closing on the woman's throat flashed in Marie's mind.

"Based on your description, we had a psychologist work with the little girl to help her recreate the crime scene. Your descriptions brought her out of shock. She made a positive I.D. of our suspect. Picked him out of a lineup. I can't tell you how thankful I am for your help. We've been trying to catch this guy for quite some time."

"Thank you very much. Now tell me the not-so-good part."
She heard him sigh.

"Some loudmouth down here at the precinct blabbed to a
reporter. It's all over the newspapers. They may start hounding
you. I'm really sorry. If it gets out of hand, give me a call.
I'll see what I can do about it."

"Thank you, Lieutenant. I appreciate that."

"It's the least I can do."

No sooner had she hung up, than the phone rang again. A
reporter. Then the doorbell rang. A news crew. Graciously,
she granted them an interview. Two more crews appeared. The
telephone rang again. Another reporter.

The novelty wore off quickly. Marie called Lieutenant
Mitchell.

Two days later the excitement passed.

One evening Marie made herself some tea and sat down to
relax when the phone rang.

"Miss Parsons?" She didn't recognize the voice and thought
it might be another reporter.

"Who's calling?"

"Sergeant Moralez, San Diego Police."

"What can I do for you, sergeant?"

"Lieutenant Mitchell told me to call. Don't open the door
for anyone. Keep your door locked and your shades drawn.
Our suspect has escaped."

"My God!"

"Stay calm. I'm on my way. I doubt he'll try anything, but
we want to make sure you're safe. I'll be there in a few minutes."

Ten minutes later, Marie heard a knock on the door. She

stood next to it for a moment and listened. "Who is it?" She said without opening.

"Sergeant Moralez."

A flood of relief filled her. "Just a minute." She undid the locks and opened the door, leaving the security chain on. "I'm sorry, sergeant. I hope you'll excuse me for asking, but may I see your badge?"

"Of course."

She reached up and felt cold metal. She ran her fingers over the badge as she had done with Lieutenant Mitchell's. The clear image of a short, dark-haired man with bristly hair and a mustache filled her mind. With a relieved sigh, she handed the badge back, then undid the security chain.

"You'll be fine," Moralez said as he stepped in. "Nothing to worry about. I'm just here as a safety precaution. I'm sure they'll recapture him shortly."

"Please come in, Sergeant. Have a seat."

"Thank you, ma'am."

She took a seat across from him after she heard him settling into the chair.

"Is it true what they say about you?" he said.

She liked the lazy sound of his voice. "I don't know. What do they say?"

"You read people's thoughts?"

"Yes, I can."

"Well.... I don't suppose, I mean — I was wondering if maybe you might...."

"Read your thoughts?"

"If it's too much trouble, don't — I mean you must be kind of nervous about the strangler and all."

"No, of course not."

"Thanks. What am I supposed to do?"

She slid her chair closer, held out her hands and placed them lightly on his head. For a moment she felt nothing, then she saw the face of the tall sandy-haired man, his blue eyes glittering like cracked ice, his thumbs pressing down on the windpipe of a policeman. The purple, bloated face of Sergeant Moralez drifted into view, followed by the faces of the women. The haunting image of the strangler's hands paralyzed her as she felt the cold fingers of her visitor sliding over her throat.

PRESTO CHANGO

David stepped into an alley and glanced over his shoulder, his dark eyes darting like those of a frightened dog. When he felt sure no one saw him, he emptied the contents of his pocket: a jackknife, a few crumpled bills, and some change. He counted thirteen dollars and twenty-nine cents, all he had left from the hundred and fifty he'd stolen from his father.

The old man had come home drunk again, knocking David's mother around. After listening to it night after night for all of his fifteen years, David couldn't bear it anymore. He waited until the old man finished the last of his Jack Daniels and dragged David's drunk mother into the bedroom. When he heard their snores, he slipped into the room and stole the wad of bills from his dad's work pants.

He had been gone for three weeks. The last time he saw himself in a mirror, his dirty blond hair looked matted and shaggy and he'd lost weight. His gaunt face and lanky body made him look older than fifteen. The collar on his flannel shirt had ripped and his Levi jacket looked greasy. One of his high-topped Converse All Stars had a hole in the toe. He stuffed the grimy bills back into his pocket and headed for the park.

He didn't want to miss The Great Mephisto's show.

Taking his usual seat in the grass, he watched the mimes and jugglers. Freckle-faced little girls in pigtails giggled at the clowns and hid behind their mothers. Ordinary dads looking ridiculous in Hawaiian shirts strolled by with their families like flocks of ducks gathering to stare and quack at the performers.

David thought about dressing up as a clown and making a fool of himself for pocket change, but what he really wanted was to be a magician — like The Great Mephisto.

He came to the park every day to watch Mephisto in hopes of learning his secrets. David had all the routines memorized but couldn't figure out the tricks. With each passing day, he realized that he couldn't learn from watching. Mephisto was much too good. David hoped to get the nerve to ask the magician to take him on as an apprentice.

He searched the jumble of people and spotted a black top hat moving through the crowd toward the fountain. His heart swelled. The people on the sidewalk parted in front of him, giving him a perfect view of Mephisto.

He looked seven feet tall in his top hat and red-lined black cape. His hair and goatee were flecked with gray and his pale blue eyes looked sharp and probing. His hat, cloak, and dark suit gave him a regal bearing. David watched him set up his table. His movements were quick, exact. Nothing wasted.

As the crowd pressed in toward the magician, David craned his neck until his gaze met Mephisto's. The old man's eyes flashed recognition. He gave a short nod. David felt a nervous smile forming on his lips.

Mephisto bowed and his white-gloved hands danced as he deftly manipulated cards, coins, and handkerchiefs. His tricks increased in complexity and his motions became more graceful and angular. A whirlwind of black and white flourished into a colorful bouquet. Bright silk handkerchiefs appeared out of nowhere. Then came his grand finale: pulling a dove out of his hat.

The crowd applauded. He gave a low bow and passed his hat. As it made the rounds his audience began to disperse until David found himself alone, facing the magician. The two studied each other a moment, then the old man beckoned with a white-gloved hand. David sidled up to him, suddenly tongue-tied.

"So, you want to be a magician," Mephisto said. His voice sounded low and velvety with a German accent.

"How did you know?" He studied an amulet that hung from the old man's neck. It looked like a real, human eye, encased in clear plastic.

"It's my business to know," Mephisto said. "I can see it in your face. You've been watching me every day. I've been waiting for you to approach me." He smiled, revealing crooked teeth.

David stared at the old man. Up close his formal suit looked worn, its cuffs frayed. The white gloves were really gray, the pants old and shiny. His eyes glittered like cracked ice and his gaze made David's stomach queasy.

"You're a runaway, aren't you?" Three eyes studied him. David forced himself to look away.

"I'm — I'm older than you think," he stammered.

"I'm sure you are, young man. Now if you're serious about learning magic, quit dawdling. Pick up that suitcase and table and follow me."

David hesitated. Mephisto gave him a sharp look, then David grabbed the suitcase and table. They walked in silence, the old man's head held high, David following two steps behind. A few blocks away, they rounded a corner onto a dead end street. The magician nodded toward a house at the end of it.

Like Mephisto, the aging Victorian structure looked stately and majestic from a distance. When they came closer, David saw peeling white paint, lopsided steps, and a sagging porch.

The front door looked battered, the foyer lit by a single low watt bulb. Mephisto led him to a small, shabbily furnished room with a dingy carpet. David looked around in wonder.

Strange symbols and yellowed pictures of snakes, dragons, and castles adorned the walls. A huge eye like the one on Mephisto's amulet was painted on the floor. A peculiar odor filled the air — the smell of crumbling plaster laced with something sour.

"Come, we'll eat," Mephisto said, speaking for the first time since they'd left the park. "Nourishment first. Then we'll speak of magic."

"I'm dying to learn." David forced himself to speak. "I've been watching you. You're awesome."

The magician nodded and motioned toward the kitchen. "Once we eat, you must tell me about yourself. Only by sharing your secrets can you hear mine. We both have many secrets, don't we?" His bushy eyebrows raised.

David followed him into the kitchen, feeling awkward. "I don't have many secrets."

"Good." Mephisto gestured toward a rickety table. David took a seat and studied the grease-streaked wall behind the crusty stove. A picture of a huge eye floating among the stars hung above the table. The rest of the walls were lined with shelves, each containing a line of jars filled with bright colored powders and liquids. Mephisto mixed some of their contents with a can of chicken noodle soup.

I wonder what he's putting in there? Should I ask? The smell of chicken soup wafted to him. His mouth watered and his stomach gurgled. *God, that smells good. Better not ask. He might get offended and make me leave.* David looked up at the picture of the eye.

"I'm sure you're wondering about that," Mephisto said when he saw David staring. "And this." He touched his amulet.

"It *is* kind of spooky."

"The sign of the brotherhood." He lowered his voice dramatically. "A secret order. I'm more than a simple magician."

David felt excitement welling inside him. "If you're not a magician," he blurted, "then what are you?"

Mephisto turned from the stove, his eyes holding David's. "A wizard."

"That's bitchin'."

The old man nodded and went back to the stove. David sat in awed silence until Mephisto ladled soup into two bowls. He thought of the powder the old man added and hesitated when the bowl was placed in front of him, but there were two bowls and they smelled *so* good.

While they ate, Mephisto quizzed him about his background. David thought he might call the cops, or worse, he might be a pervert. He felt nervous and unsure, but the warm soup relaxed him. The more he ate, the more comfortable he became until he found himself volunteering information that the magician hadn't even asked for.

"My mom and dad don't get along too good. They like to drink, but it makes them fight. If I'm around, my dad hits me. I got sick of it."

"Well, David." Mephisto pushed back from the table. "It looks like you might be the one I've been waiting for. I'll take you on as an apprentice on a trial basis." He paused "The magic you've seen is not as simple as it seems. It takes great dedication."

More than ever, David wanted to be taught by the old man. "I'm ready. I'll do whatever you want. Anything." He yawned.

Mephisto leaned back in his chair, eyes narrowed, hand stroking his beard. "Anything?"

"Name it."

"There are secret rituals that must be performed before the acolyte can approach the inner circle." Mephisto's eyes glazed. He turned his head to the side as if listening to someone talking, then nodded. "Yes, you can stay with us — I mean me. If you prove yourself worthy, I will initiate you."

His words sounded funny. Fuzzy. David shook his head. His eyes felt heavy. He had been so intent on eating his own soup, he hadn't noticed Mephisto not eating his.

"You can sleep in the sacred chamber." The voice seemed to be drifting.

Sacred chamber? What does he mean? "But what about you?" he mumbled. "You haven't told me about yourself." David's head drooped, then his eyes jerked open. His vision grew hazy.

"Come along now." David felt the magician dragging him up from the chair. He struggled to stand, but his knees buckled.

His mouth fell open and his words blurred into a moan.

"Save your energy. You need your strength for the trial. Don't fight. Go with it." He felt Mephisto's moist, sour breath tickling his neck, the whisper echoing until it turned into the sound of his own breathing. A chill rolled up the nape of his neck. He gave in and let sleep take him.

In his dreams, he heard two people arguing and thought he was back at home. He couldn't make out the words, only the high raspy sound of one voice. The other sounded low, relaxed. Mephisto. He awoke in darkness, head throbbing dully, mouth dry. A dank mildewy smell filled the air. He sat up and tried to get his bearings by sliding his hand along the mattress behind him until he felt a padded wall.

A rush of adrenaline jolted him fully awake. *What the hell?* He swung his legs over the side of the cot, then moved across the floor, sliding his feet until he reached the opposite wall. Padded.

Moving to his right, he felt his way along the wall. When he came to a doorway a flood of relief filled him. He pushed open the door and slipped through. His leg hit something hard. He reached down and touched cold porcelain. A toilet. Two more steps took him to a sink and another wall.

Not really sure of his aim in the dark, he relieved himself, then stepped back into the padded room, sliding along the wall, turning at each corner until he counted four. No doors, no windows. Only padding. Sweat slid down his back and neck, trickling into his armpits.

His panic rose, peaking into hopelessness, then collapsing into smoldering frustration. "Son-of-a-bitch." His voice sounded strange. Small. "Son-of-a-bitch," he said louder, his voice trembling somewhere between fear and anger. "Son-of-a-bitch!" he screamed punching the wall. The walls sucked up the sound of his voice and the thuds of his punches; as if his fists had struck the padded lid of a giant coffin. He put his face in his hands and cried himself to sleep.

Voices. Distant. Muffled. He put his ear to the wall, but still couldn't make out the words. He thought he could hear the voices better close to the bathroom. Stepping inside, he put his ear against the cold plaster of the unpadded wall and heard shuffling noises like furniture being moved, then the voices.

"Are we going to sacrifice him?" The first voice sounded strained, as if on the verge of erupting.

"No," the second voice answered. It sounded low and in control, yet defensive. Mephisto.

"A sacrifice is needed. Through new blood we grow."

David's chest tightened. His stomach felt cold and hollow.

"Out of the question," Mephisto said.

David breathed a sigh of relief.

"What do you mean, out of the question? You haven't lost your nerve, have you?"

"This one's different. He's, he's...." The words hung in the air, then he spoke again, his voice breathless. "I think he's the chosen one."

"The chosen one?" The grainy voice reminded David of a Gestapo torturer in old war movies.

"I've already begun the initiation rites. If he passes, we can consecrate him. Teach him the secret arts. Mephisto's voice rose steadily, an air of conviction bleeding through every word. "As it is written in the great book: 'Behold, the acolyte will

appear and the keeper will sense his desire. The ritual will
come to pass and a new age will spring forth'."

"What if you're wrong?"

"The initiation will tell us that."

"And if he fails?"

"We have another sacrifice."

A chill clambered across David's scalp like a spider. Was
he being held by the members of an insane cult or was he being
tested by a benevolent wizard?

Common sense told him the former was true, but his sanity
and hope hinged on the latter. He shuffled back to his cot and
lay down, hands clasped behind his head, mind racing in time
with the heartbeat pounding in his ears. Hunger gnawed at his
gut, a burrowing parasite worming its way to his core, robbing
him of vitality. How long had he been here? When was the
last time he ate? He thought of the Big Mac and shake he had
the day before. After a long drink at the bathroom tap, he slept
and dreamed of ancient temples and robed priests drinking
blood as they performed secret rituals.

Bright red pierced his brain. His eyes fluttered open burning
an image of the dark outline of Mephisto filling a doorway, his
cape spread wide like Dracula. The light brought excruciating
pain. David scrunched his eyes shut.

"Let me out of here!" he shrieked.

"I know you must be angry." Mephisto's velvety words gave
David strange comfort. "You said you wanted to be a magician.
I am only preparing you."

David thought of the conversation he had listened to through
the wall but was afraid to let the old man know he'd overheard.
"What do you mean preparing me? You're starving me!"

"I've brought nourishment, but you must eat slowly. Otherwise, you'll be sick."

"I don't want to be a magician anymore."

"You are the chosen one the great book speaks of. You have been picked from among thousands by the Almighty."

"What book are you talking about?"

"The Ancient Book of Secret and Forbidden Knowledge. It's been passed down to me by my Druidic forefathers."

David tried to open his eyes, but the light hurt too much. He heard the muffled thud of the door, and the room went dark again. "Turn on the god-damned lights!" he screamed.

No answer.

The enticing aroma of food drifted to him. His mouth watered. He crawled across the floor toward the door and the smell grew stronger. He slid his hand back and forth on the floor in front of him. It hit something — a warm plate — something breaded, fried, a little greasy. He grabbed at it.

Remembering Mephisto's warning, he chewed slowly, the watering in his mouth so intense it hurt. Chicken. He ate more, pacing himself — savoring each bite, tasting different kinds of meat. Different shapes. Different textures. Peas and carrots. Then his fingers found a glass of milk. He drank a sip at a time.

His felt his strength return. He licked the plate clean and drank the last of his milk for dessert, then went to the bathroom, put his ear to the wall, and listened.

"He's not going to make it." The higher, grating voice said.

"Give the boy a chance," Mephisto answered.

"He's had his chance. He doesn't want to learn. It's time for the initiation or else give him up as a sacrifice."

"And if I refuse?"

45

"I'll take things into my own hands. *I* will not hesitate to perform the sacrifice. Through new blood, we grow."

David backed away from the wall. His stomach felt cold and sour. Panic nipped at his brain. He thrust his hand into his pocket. His fingers closed around his jackknife. He put his ear to the wall and listened.

No sound.

He jabbed at the plaster with the knife, pausing every few minutes to listen, digging. He dug until he came across wood slats. He widened the hole, finally pushing his knife all the way through. When he had a big enough hole, he put his eye to it. More blackness.

"Shit. Where does it go?" He dug frantically, until he had a hole wide enough to crawl through. Only the wood slats blocked him. He thought of kicking through but feared he would be heard.

He carved the tops, then the bottoms of each slat, thinning them, then pushing. Each one gave way with a snap that sounded alarmingly loud. Soon, he had a hole big enough for his head and shoulders.

He thrust his head into the darkness and saw a tiny spot of light a few feet from his face. A keyhole. He wriggled through the wall, his hopes of escape rising until he heard the sound of footsteps.

He jerked his head back. The point of a jutting slat stabbed into the back of his skull. He winced, pushed forward and drew his head back slowly.

Bolting from the bathroom, he landed back on the cot as the door to his room opened. He closed his eyes to the blinding light and touched the back of his head. A warm trickle ran between his fingers. He choked back tears and listened. Only the sound of breathing. His and someone else's. The door closed.

The voices started again, louder because of the hole in the wall and louder for another reason: an argument. He couldn't make out what they were saying, but he knew the sounds of a fight.

The voices grew quiet, then the door to his room opened. The smell of food. The door closed. He found the tray and a repeat of his last meal. This time he wolfed it down.

He finished and sat on the cot, ears vigilant. When he heard nothing, he crept to the bathroom and eased himself through the hole in the wall, staying on his hands and knees to explore the room. He didn't have to go far. He'd escaped into a closet. He groped for the door, his sweaty palm sliding over the knob. His heart fluttered. He held his breath, tightened his grip, and turned. Locked. He bit his tongue to keep from screaming.

After calming himself, he found a light switch, scrunched his eyes shut and flicked it. The light burned, making his first impressions hazy, then things drifted into focus. Shelves lined with jars. Things floating in them. He stepped closer.

His stomach knotted.

Eyeballs floated in one. Ears in another. Fingers. Strips of flesh. He thought of his meals eaten in the dark and his stomach spasmed as his last meal splattered against the door. His mind raced aimlessly, building to a crescendo until he blacked out.

When he opened his eyes, horror greeted him. Shelf upon shelf of lifeless terror, poised in silent repose. Sightless eyes staring vacantly, ears that didn't hear his bubbling sobs.

Motionless fingers beckoning him away from sanity.

Bile burned in his throat. Whimpering, he pushed himself further into the corner where he spied a battered steamer trunk covered with decals from all over the world. The Great Mephisto had been stenciled on it in faded silver paint. David shuddered when he thought about what might be in it. On a sudden impulse, he grabbed the lid and flipped it open.

Cards, brightly colored handkerchiefs, a top hat, a cape, a cane, large silver rings and mysterious boxes filled the trunk. Some of the tricks David recognized, others he'd never seen. Two books lay in one corner: "One Thousand and One Magic Tricks" and "The Ancient Book of Secret and Forbidden Knowledge." David felt as though he watched himself from a distance as his hand picked up the second book.

Childlike scribbles in different colored crayon filled the first pages. Crude pictures. Disembodied eyes and men in dark, hooded robes. Men lying on tables. Hooded men standing over them with bloody knives. For the most part, the scrawls were illegible, but here and there he could make out a word.

New Blood. Feeding. Passage. And German words: *"Der Geist, der stets verneint".* Beneath it the words: "The spirit who always negates. Through new blood, we grow."

The hairs bristled on his scalp.

He flipped to the second part of the album. Scores of newspaper articles dating back close to seventy years. The stories were all basically the same.

BODY PARTS FOUND, PIECES STILL MISSING
SHALLOW GRAVE REVEALS DISFIGURED BODIES
CULT ACTIVITY SUSPECTED
HUNT STILL ON FOR MANCHESTER MANGLER

The most recent article had a page to itself.

MUTILATION SUSPECT ESCAPES FROM INSTITUTION

The face looked younger and clean-shaven, but David recognized Mephisto. His body grew cold. He heard a tiny noise and looked up to see the doorknob twisting. His stomach wrenched.

The door opened on squeaking hinges and David looked up into the glistening eyes of Mephisto boring into him from beneath a black hooded cloak. His mind told him to jump up and run past the old man, but his body remained on the floor, a quivering mass.

"You've discovered the truth," Mephisto said quietly. "Now the initiation must proceed."

David's mouth hung open in a silent scream. He was dimly aware of the string of saliva running down his chin onto the book. Mephisto pulled him to his feet, half dragging him into another room, talking to him in a calm, even voice that drove the fear deeper into David with each word.

"A good magician has many talents, among them the skills of an escape artist. You've proven yourself worthy."

Black rooms and bizarre red symbols jumped out at him. A single crimson eye covered one wall. A tiny red altar sat below it. Candles flickered, bathing the room in dancing uneven light.

David hung limp in the old magician's arms until he felt himself dragged up onto the altar, then his adrenaline raced. He struggled, trying to get his jackknife. Mephisto produced a cloth and pressed it over David's nose and mouth.

He coughed, remembering the ether smell from the time his

tonsils had been removed. He let go of the knife, pulled his hand out, tried to hit Mephisto and coughed again. The sound echoed. Candlelight glittered in Mephisto's eyes.

Voices. Chanting. Foreign sounding words. The grainy, straining voice. The man who'd been arguing with Mephisto. "*Der Geist, der stets verneint.*"

David found himself tied to the altar. He expected many faces but saw only one hooded figure kneeling in front of the altar holding a butcher knife high in front of him like a priest bearing a cross. The figure looked up, and David locked eyes with Mephisto.

The magician smiled and rose.

"You awaken," he said, his voice low, silken. "It is good. The acolyte must witness the passage."

David strained against his bonds. "You're nuts," he said between gritted teeth. "Let me go, you fucking lunatic!"

Something behind the old man's eyes shifted. His face contorted.

"Through new blood, we grow," the strained, raspy voice said through Mephisto's mouth. He raised the knife over his head. The gold shimmer of candlelight glinted off the blade. Mephisto turned his head to the side as if studying David. His eyes looked soft, imploring. He paused, then brought the knife down hard, cutting his own throat.

David let out a startled cry and shut his eyes. Hot coppery crimson spurted onto him, finding its way into his mouth and nose along with a dark alien presence that fluttered through his consciousness like a bat.

*　　*　　*　　*　　*

With a flourish of his hands and a flap of his cape, David produced the bouquet. The crowd of youngsters applauded. His movements weren't as deft as those of his mentor, but he improved every day. The beginnings of a goatee formed on his chin, but his youth made the peach-fuzz almost invisible.

When his show ended and the hat had been passed, he packed his things. A disheveled younger boy who had come to watch again studied him from a distance. Third day in a row.

David peered over his shoulder, his eyes meeting those of the other, locking for a moment.

Young, he thought. *Probably a runaway. I'll bet he wants to learn magic.*

PARTS

Jesus, the old dude wasn't kidding when he said this crate runs a little rough," Eric Hart muttered. He fiddled with the carburetor linkage and the whole car shuddered in a mechanical version of a petit mal seizure. "Feels like something's sticking somewhere."

The engine coughed and sputtered, then the carb made a deep sucking sound before the engine jumped into high revs. The sudden blast of air from the fan blew Eric's hair into his face. A moment later the car jerked into a grand mal spasm, then died.

He pushed the hair out of his eyes and stepped back, admiring the old hearse. A gleaming silver '63 Caddy with a black vinyl top. Cherry, if not for the engine problem. Though the car acted strange, he had no doubt he'd find what was wrong. Eric had a way with cars.

He wiped his finger on his sleeve before caressing the fender. "Nothing I can't fix, old girl. That's why you ended up here. Everyone in town knows I'm the best." He pulled a rag from the back pocket of his coveralls and wiped the grease off his hands before leaning into the front seat to restart the engine.

Red idiot lights glared at him from the dashboard and the

cloying smell from decades of dying flowers assaulted his nostrils. "Even has a built-in perpetual air freshener." He chuckled and reached toward the ignition. The engine jumped briefly to life and the visor over the driver's side flopped down, exposing a faded chauffeur's license.

Eric blinked in surprise. *Damn thing has a mind of its own. Better take a closer look at the carb then check the timing.* He shut off the ignition and eyed the yellowing picture on the license.

The old guy had come into the Shell station that morning, dapper in his somber gray suit. He looked like a cross between Albert Einstein and Mark Twain with his snow-white hair, full mustache, and bushy eyebrows. Dark eyes, half sad, half amused, peered out from the drawn skin of his face. His wry smile looked feral when thin lips revealed crooked yellow teeth like weathered gravestones.

"Damndest thing," the old man said, his expression going deadpan. "Brought this thing to three different mechanics. None of 'em could fix it. Wouldn't work on it. All they said was it needed parts."

"Sure is a beauty," Eric said. "Don't know why anybody wouldn't want to work on her. Should have 'er ready by this afternoon."

"Good." A flash of headstone teeth.

With the engine off, Eric went back to work under the hood, inspecting the carburetor linkage. He couldn't see anything out of the norm until he moved the linkage assembly back and forth with his hand. *Something's* making this baby bind. He worked the linkage some more, feeling for the trouble spot, then scanned its length until he saw something black about an inch and a half long, stuck in the linkage near the firewall. "Bingo!"

Reaching down, he plucked the object from its resting place. It felt spongy like a gasket or grommet, and one edge of it felt rough. He didn't recognize its triangular shape. When he held it up to the light, he saw it had a rounded tip, and two holes. Some kind of valve? He shrugged and set it aside, directing his attention back to the engine.

She should run smoother now. He gave the linkage a once over. Then on instinct, he checked the choke assembly. Working one of the rods, he saw that it too had something jamming its movement. "Damn," he muttered. Another blackened object blocked the choke. "A wonder this thing ever ran."

He examined his find on the end of his screwdriver. This one felt soft and spongy too, but it had a different shape. Might be a piece of collapsed hose, but where did it come from? It looked long, flat, and thick with a smooth oval indent on one side.

"Weird shit."

He put his second find next to the first and continued his inspection, scrutinizing each part with care. He didn't see anything else. Might as well crank her up and see what she does." He stepped back, wiping his hands.

When he turned the key, the engine roared to life, sputtered and coughed before settling into a spastic idle. Eric went to the front of the car, plugged in the timing light and checked the timing. Perfect. He tried adjusting the idle mixture screw. The engine shuddered and died.

One of the jets? Turning off the key, he pushed open the butterfly plate on the carburetor and looked down inside with his flashlight. "What the hell?"

This time he found a small purplish-black ball about three quarters of an inch in diameter stuck between one of the jets and the intake barrel. Eric grabbed his needle-nose pliers and pulled it out. Black strings trailed along the end of it.

"Don't know what the hell it is, but I'll bet it's what's been giving me all this grief." He tossed it next to the other two things he'd found and restarted the car with no problems. After fine-tuning the carburetor, it idled perfectly. He revved it a few times, smiling at the smooth sound of the big V8.

Eric killed the engine and eyed his findings, wondering what they were. Filling an old coffee can with gas, he dumped the black pieces into it, swirled them around, then let them soak while he grabbed a bite to eat.

Forty-five minutes later, he tilted the coffee can to one side and gawked in disbelief at the vacuous stare of an eyeball regarding him from the bottom of the can. A ham and cheese on rye and two Budweisers promptly exited his body the same way they'd gone in.

When the nausea passed, he cleaned up his mess and steeled himself for another peek in the can. Holding it at arm's length, he dumped its contents into a strainer at the back of the shop. The eyeball tumbled out first. Things he now recognized as a piece of an ear and the end of a nose followed.

Eric gagged, but nothing remained in his stomach. His skin felt hot and prickly. He wiped sweat from his forehead and shook off the chill that scrambled across his scalp like a spider. His first reaction was to call the cops, but he forced his panic back. Instead, he went to the office to think things out.

No, he wouldn't call the cops. Not yet. He'd call the old

guy first. Have him come get his car. Watch for a reaction. See how he acted. *Then* he'd call the cops.

He made the call, gathered up the eye, ear, and nose with his pliers and gingerly wrapped them in a clean rag which he set on the front fender. While waiting for the old man, he studied the Caddy. Its front hood hung open like the jaw of an alligator lying in wait. Another chill danced down his spine.

The old man showed up twenty minutes later, looking as dapper as he had that morning.

"I found the problem," Eric said, watching him closely.

Nothing.

"I think you might be interested in seeing what caused the trouble."

"If you think it's important."

Eric led him into the repair bay. The old man waited patiently as Eric unwrapped the eye, ear, and nose. The old man looked at him, his expression unchanged. "Where did you find these?"

Eric nodded toward the engine then leaned over the fender. "I found the first part here." He pointed at the linkage down by the firewall. "The nose. And the second part of the ear, here." He laid a hand on the choke assembly and looked back at the old man. No reaction. He turned back to the car. "I found the eyeball blocking one of the jets in the carb." He pushed down on the butterfly plate and stuck his hand in the carburetor.

The car suddenly roared to life and the choke plate slammed shut. Eric opened his mouth, howling as he felt the end of his finger nipped off at the joint. He watched in horror as the carburetor sucked it down with a "thwup." He jerked back and the hood slammed down on his head.

As the blur of the whirling fan rushed toward his face, he

could hear the old man. "Tsk, tsk. I guess it really *does* need parts. Same thing happened to the other three mechanics."

NO CHOICE

The rain tapped steadily against the window, sluicing down the panes. Pale yellow from the streetlight outside shone through the moving water making shifting patterns of shadow and light around the room. Amanda huddled in bed, her limp brown hair cascading haphazardly over the comforter she clutched around slight shoulders. She stared at the barren walls of her apartment while her body convulsed with sobs. Tears ran down her cheeks.

"I killed him," she whispered. "Killed my baby. Oh God, how can you forgive me?"

As if answering her plea, the wind gusted and the rain beat harder. Her breath caught and for a moment she thought she heard the wail of an infant before realizing that the eerie cry came from the wind whistling around the eaves.

Amanda put her face in her hands. The images rushed back to her as they had so many times since it happened. She had felt so vulnerable lying nude in the examination room, the cold, clinical steel of the stirrups spreading her legs, exposing her. No protection except a flimsy sheet draped over her from the knees up. The only warmth came from a big light pointing down below the sheet where she couldn't see what was happening.

How routine it had all been to the doctor and nurse. No show of sympathy. No support while she went through a maelstrom of emotions, wondering. Wondering.

"Is this really the right thing?" she blurted. "Can't there be another way?"

"There are no alternatives." The doctor shook his head. His face showed no expression. "You've seen the test results. Your life is in danger."

"If I do this, I'll *never* be able to have a baby."

"And if you don't, the chances are great that you'll die. The damage done to your uterus in the past has made your condition critical." He turned to the side and picked something up from a tray. A moment later she felt him pushing his hands into her.

She wanted to stop him when he did something that pinched inside her (an injection?), but the words caught in her throat. No turning back now.

"Relax," he said in a monotone. "It'll be over in a couple of minutes." Then he left the room.

Twenty minutes later he came back. She saw the flash of something long and silver. A moment later she felt the cold metal working its way deep inside her like some insidious alien probe burrowing its way into the root of her being. The doctor shook the instrument, moved it around, and shook it again. Amanda panicked and hyperventilated when she felt her insides being pulled on, then she felt the sickening sensation of part of her being sucked out. She heard a muffled sound from somewhere inside her like air rushing into a newly opened jar and experienced a brief moment of emptiness before the guilt rushed in, filling the vacuum left by the absence of the tiny life that had lived in her.

When the doctor and nurse left the room, her emotions flew wildly, cutting through her like shattering glass. She cried with no sense of relief and tried to blot out the memory, but couldn't erase the feeling of the fetus being sucked out. Every time she closed her eyes she relived the moment.

The storm gusted, rattling her apartment window. She heard the cry in the wind again. So much like an infant. Amanda jerked her head up and a slow chill clambered down her spine. She reached for her sleeping pills, took a few, then lay back on the bed fighting off the nightmarish images that assaulted her until the blackness swallowed her, allowing her to escape into oblivion. She slept deep and dreamless until the effect of the pills lessened and she drifted back where dreams and memories mingled, waiting for her attention.

Fourteen again and pregnant for the first time. Billy, her first love who seemed so grown up at seventeen had talked her into "going all the way." Her first experience with sex and she'd become pregnant. She knew Billy couldn't provide for her, but she wanted the baby more than anything she could ever remember wanting. She knew she could learn to take care of it.

Then her father found out.

Five days later he flew her to a clinic someplace in New York where they took her baby from her. In comparison to the impersonal, clinical sterility of her most recent experience, her first time had been crude — the doctor insensitive and uncaring. She came out of it with an infection that lingered for months.

She heard the cry of an infant from another part of her mind and remembered the wind whistling around the building. It suddenly changed pitch so it sounded as if there were two of them. She shook her head to rouse herself and felt something weighing on her, as if her whole body were covered with a lead-lined sheet that pressed her deeper into the mattress.

When she came awake, the sounds of the cries seemed to hover about her for a moment before fading, then a scattering of raindrops pattered across the window followed by silence. She forced herself to sit up and peer out into the grayness. A thick fog rolled in, bringing with it billowing mists that slid along the side of the building.

From out of the silence, Amanda thought she heard the cry of the wind again, then realized it had stopped. Senses poised, she listened intently. From somewhere in the distance she heard it again. Barely audible, yet distinct. She had no doubt in her mind that it *was* the cry of an infant — no two! Two babies crying! She turned her head to the side trying to determine where the cries came from. No matter which way she turned, it sounded the same. She hurried to the other room to see if the tiny voices would change, but the volume remained constant. She thought maybe they might be coming from outside her apartment so she tip-toed to the door, undid the lock and cracked it open. No change.

"Hearing things," she mumbled and shuffled back to bed. The crying didn't stop. How can they let them cry like that? she wondered. Why doesn't the mother check on them? They need attention.

She put her hands over her ears but could still hear the tiny wailing of their voices. The sound made her want to scream. She eyed the bottle of pills on her dresser, shook some into her hand and swallowed them, then lay back under her comforter and closed her eyes to wait for the peace that only sleep could bring.

Somewhere between wakefulness and slumber the crying stopped, but its insistence triggered another memory. New images flooded her mind. Amanda at twenty-three, pregnant and wanting the baby, knowing she was old enough and responsible enough to care for it. Ken, not really wanting it, but staying with her, being supportive. Amanda taking care of herself, eating the right things, working to stay healthy. In the beginning, everything went well until she began having morning sickness. She tried eating more, but to her horror she couldn't hold food down. Her weight dropped and she became dehydrated.

The doctor kept her in the hospital and put her on IV's, frequently checking her eyes. Her condition deteriorated. After her fourth eye examination, his manner changed. She knew by the look on his face that the situation had become critical.

"What is it?" she said. "What's wrong?"

"Your weight is still dropping." He said, flipping through her chart. "And your life is in danger. We're going to have to terminate the pregnancy."

Amanda felt as if she had been punched in the stomach. "What?" she gasped. "Abort it?"

"I'm sorry. You have a condition called Hyperemesis Gravidarum. This pregnancy could kill you. "

"Hyper what? Give it to me in English."

"Starvation. I'm not sure what caused it, but it may be related to the infection you had after your first abortion. I don't know, and I don't have the time to find out."

Ken stayed with her through the whole ordeal. Sweet and supportive. After the abortion he slipped out of her life and disappeared, leaving Amanda alone again.

Her most recent loss came back to her. The doctor pushing

his hands into her, the flash of cold metal and her insides being pulled on followed by the sickening sensation of part of her being sucked out, a muffled sound inside her, then emptiness and guilt rushing in, following her down into the waiting darkness.

She opened her eyes and waited to hear the crying babies. Complete silence enveloped her like the thick mist that pressed against the window, suffocating the building. She felt as if an unseen part of the mist had made its way into the room and thrown itself over her like an invisible shroud. Her grief had become a dull throb, that strained to send yet another pulse of muted sorrow through her being. She lay immobile in the stillness trying to fathom it.

The answer came in a sudden gust of wind. A cacophony of infant cries, childish voices, and whispers, all spiraling through her mind. When the initial shock passed, she understood.

"Mommy," the oldest whispered. "Mommy, hug me, I'm scared." A newborn infant bawled and a little girl whispered that she was lonely and wanted someone to play with.

"Where are you?" Amanda cried. "Where are you?"

"Here."

The little voice sounded as if it were in the apartment with her. In the next room. Amanda forced herself to sit up and thought she saw a tiny figure darting past the door. "Who's there?"

"Mommy, hug me, I'm scared."

Fear swept through her, then curiosity. Amanda stood on trembling legs and took a tentative step toward the doorway. Her heart raced. In a burst of determination, she crossed the threshold into the other room.

The apartment door sat open, its inner latch undone. Delicate fingers of mist crept along the floor into the apartment. She saw no one. The possibility of neighbor children playing a prank crossed her mind, but they couldn't have undone the latch from inside.

The voices came again from out in the hall, louder than before. She knew there were three. Instinctively, she went in the direction of the mist, following the voices which always seemed to be slightly ahead. The mist thickened and she saw a vague form disappearing furtively around a corner up ahead. "Don't run, honey," she heard herself saying. "Mommy's coming."

She rounded the corner. The sound of little feet scampered up the stairs. The voices grew louder, more insistent: the infant's cries impatient and demanding.

Mist billowed down the stairway like a smoky waterfall. Amanda hurried and ascended the stairs, stepping out onto the roof into a surreal whiteness that covered the murky landscape. A small, dark form floated in the mist. She glanced down at her feet and saw tendrils of mist snaking around her ankles, as if beckoning her forward into the shadows. The wind kicked up, bringing with it the plaintive utterances of her children. A sprinkling of raindrops peppered her face, mixing with her tears.

She looked up and saw a forest spread out before her. The mists parted, revealing a path to the top of a mountain. She made her way along it until she could see the tiny forms awaiting her. Then she began to run.

She came to a cliff at the end of the path where she paused to listen. The voices of the children stopped, their forms gone. A wall of mist hovered beyond the edge of the precipice and though she heard no cries, Amanda felt her babies beckoning.

64

The wind blew, the rains came, and Amanda stepped over the edge. As she plummeted toward the sidewalk, she felt a swelling of unbounded joy and a blissful completeness she had never thought possible. At last, she would be where she belonged. With her children.

THE SMALL DARK ROOM OF THE SOUL

*V*asquez watched the fat bearded gringo hold the tiny head by its hair and slowly twirl it in front of him. In spite of the moist, rot-smelling jungle air pressing in like the semi-darkness of the cantina, he could still smell the gringo's sweat.

The American grunted and tossed the head onto the table. "Counterfeit. Not even a good one."

Vasquez took a sip of rum and fingered his knife while eyeing the sack of doubloons on the table next to the man's musket. Maybe he would cut this fat pig's throat and take his gold. "What do you mean, counterfeit? It's a real head, is it not?"

The pig grunted. "It's real, but it's probably been stolen from an unclaimed corpse at the hospital or the body of a peasant."

Vasquez cringed at the mention of the dead. His daughter's face filled his thoughts. If he had only listened to her cries.... He downed his rum and poured another cup. "But look at the workmanship." He picked up the head, thrust it toward the gringo and pointed. "You can barely see the slit in the back. Have you ever seen anything so neat?"

The American frowned. "That's my point." He took the head and put his finger on its neck. "The incision in a legitimate Jivaro

66

tsantsa is drawn together with coarse fiber."

He turned the head face out. It looked angry as if it were scowling; then he dropped it onto the table and made a dismissive gesture. "My clients are from prestigious universities and pay good money for the real thing."

Vasquez grabbed the head, spit on the table and turned to leave. To hell with this fat American pig. There were plenty of other buyers, ones who didn't know the difference. He'd find another way to get rum money. He stumbled out of the cantina. Anything to stay drunk and keep from facing Maria's death, only now he was stuck with a load of heads which he'd be forced to peddle on the street. Maybe he could make enough to pay off Rodrigo and buy his heads directly from one of those crazy Indians. Maybe he could pay them to show him how they shrunk the heads? He could make his own counterfeits. No more being the middle man.

He sold his heads at a lower price to another peddler, bought two bottles of rum and went in search of Rodrigo. He found his childhood friend on the outskirts of the village at the forest's edge.

Rodrigo leaned back on two legs of a chair against the wall on the inside of an old decaying hut. A small tin cup of rum sat in front of him on a battered wooden table. His sombrero tilted forward, partially covering a scar that ran from his left eyelid to his chin.

"*Amigo!*" Vasquez held up a jug of rum. "I've been looking all over for you. I have some business to discuss. Share a drink?"

Rodrigo pushed his cup toward Vasquez who sat down, filled it and took a swig from the bottle. A plump rat scurried across one of the roof timbers and disappeared through a hole in the thatch. Rodrigo smiled at it, then leveled his gaze at Vasquez. "You wish to buy more *tsantsas*, amigo?"

Vasquez wiped sweat from his eyes and dropped two sacks of doubloons on the table. "No more counterfeits."

"It's what the Indians give me."

Vasquez knew Rodrigo was lying. Anyone could get counterfeits. He nodded toward the doubloons. "Take me to the Indians. Let me make my own deal."

Except for a momentary flicker in his eyes, Rodrigo's expression remained unchanged. "I'll supply all you want."

Vasquez looked down at his hands. "But I want to ...." He saw a flash of metal, then a machete slammed into the table between the two bags. Slivers of wood flew. The quivering blade swayed inches from his finger. He looked into Rodrigo's eyes and saw nothing but two pieces of flint.

"I said I'll supply all you want."

Vasquez felt his face grow hot as fear and rage swept through him. "That's okay with me, amigo." He snatched up his gold and rum so Rodrigo would not see his shaking hands. "I'll be back when you are in a better mood." He turned and started toward the door.

"Vasquez!"

He stopped but didn't turn.

"You drink too much."

"*Pinche!* " He stormed out of the hut toward the center of town. In spite of a light breeze, the air still felt thick and moist on his face. The damp, rotting vegetable smell of the nearby rain forest pressed in on him. He'd known Rodrigo since they'd been boys. There was no reason for him to treat an old friend like that....

A little girl's scream pierced the air.

"Maria!"

A bolt of anguish shot through him, followed by the image of a small, darkened room. Maria was gone. He ran in the direction of the cry and saw two ragged, dark-haired boys trying to take a little girl's doll. "Hey, you there! Leave her alone!" Frightened eyes looked up at him, then the boys darted into an alley leaving a disheveled little girl alone clutching her tattered doll. Tears streaked her dirt smudged face.

Vasquez felt as if a cold fist had been driven into his stomach. His heart swelled. "Ah, little *senorita*, your baby has been hurt." He pressed a doubloon into her tiny hand. "Take her to the doctor." The girl stared wide-eyed at the coin, then scampered off.

He gazed down the darkened alley and remembered Maria's cries from the storeroom, then the screaming that had turned to sobs, finally fading to silence. He thought she'd cried herself to sleep, but it hadn't been sleep.

He filled his mind with the thought of Rodrigo. Fresh, hot anger replaced sorrow. He liked the way it made him feel. Strong. To hell with Rodrigo. If he did not want to share his secret, then his friend would find the secret for himself.

He took a roundabout path through the village back streets and approached Rodrigo's from the side. Settling himself between the roots of a huge tree, he watched the hut and the trail that disappeared into the forest behind it. A steady stream of street peddlers moved in and out, most bringing gold and leaving with shrunken heads and other artifacts. The last two men brought long, heavy cloth-wrapped items that looked suspiciously like dead bodies.

As the afternoon sun cast the forest into lines and angles of shadow, Vasquez hugged the base of a tree and watched his friend emerge from the hut. When Rodrigo seemed satisfied that no one watched him, he went back in and came out with two muskets and a burro. The cloth-wrapped items were slung across its back. Rodrigo started down the forest path, passing within a few feet of Vasquez through a thick grove of trees. Vasquez followed from a safe distance as Rodrigo walked another mile or so to a steep river bank, followed it for awhile before crossing into a small clearing. By now the forest had grown darker. Vasquez stayed hidden in the growing shadows by the clearing's edge.

A movement in the bushes made his heart jump, then an Indian carrying a spear and a large shield emerged from the shadows on the other side of the clearing. Vasquez pulled out a bottle and gulped rum.

Tall and well-proportioned, the Indian wore a long skirt and a wide belt made of hair. A beautiful red band decorated with spangles of shell encircled his head. His voice sounded fierce and arrogant. "You have the guns and the dead. I have more *tsantsas.*"

Rodrigo handed the rifles to the Indian and pulled the bodies from the burro. The Indian waved toward the forest. Two more Indians stepped into the clearing and set a net full of shrunken heads at Rodrigo's feet. Rodrigo picked up the net and the Indians faded back into the surrounding vegetation.

Vasquez dropped lower to the ground as Rodrigo passed then followed him out of the forest. By the time they reached the village edge, a full moon had risen. To hell with that pig

Rodrigo. Who needed him? Vasquez would make his own deal.

The next day, he used his gold to buy five muskets, four of which he bundled and strapped to his back. The fifth he kept loaded and ready. He went into the forest early with his bundle of goods and two jugs of rum to wait for Rodrigo and the Indians. When the sun had all but disappeared, they came again and made another deal.

When Rodrigo went his way, Vasquez hurried around to the edge of the clearing to catch the Indians before the forest swallowed them again. He wanted to call out but held back for fear of alerting Rodrigo. He stumbled ahead, sweat stinging his eyes and the undergrowth tugging at his clothes. When he looked up a few moments later, the Indians had disappeared.

"*Pinche!*"

He set down his load and dropped onto his back, his hands cradling the one loaded musket. His breath came in short gasps. The buzz of insects filled his ears. The forest had darkened. He closed his eyes, opened them, and gazed up into the fierce eyes of an Indian. "*Amigo.*" His throat suddenly felt dry. "You speak my language?"

Out of the corner of his eye he saw two more Indians. He pointed to the bundle of guns. "*Tsantsas.* You show me? I bring more guns — plenty more. Teach me how to shrink the heads."

The Indian's eyes narrowed, then he nodded. The other two men picked up the guns and the three started back toward the fading sun. Vasquez scrambled to his feet and followed.

By the time darkness shrouded the forest, they came to the river. The three Indians sat and talked quietly in their native tongue. They seemed aware of Vasquez, but no one acknowledged his presence. He sat off to the side clutching his gun, muttering and drinking rum until he lost consciousness.

He awoke to noises in the brush. Gray dawn filled his senses. His companions grew quiet as a single line of Indians carrying spears and baskets came out of the forest on the other side of the river. They set up campfires and a temporary shelter on a sand bar.

Vasquez stationed himself by the corner of the shelter and nervously sipped rum while the Indians removed leaf-wrapped heads from their baskets, each holding up a respective prize and peeling leaves away. Ragged muscle and tendon dangled from severed necks. Blood that looked black and viscous in the orange glow of the firelight dripped from the strips of flesh. Vasquez fought back the rising bile in his throat, turned away and tried to wash the bitterness down with rum.

When he turned back, an older, gaunt-faced indian sat down beside him. Dark, solemn eyes studied him intently. Vasquez couldn't look at the man's piercing gaze, so he turned back to the morbid scene before him.

"It is the enemy," the old man said.

Vasquez jumped at the sound of his voice. No one had spoken to him since the three Indians had first taken his guns.

The warriors made slits in the back of each head and skinned them from the skulls, the same way trappers removed the skins from rabbits. They scraped meat from the inside, fastened the eyelids shut and reversed the skin so the head formed a sack with the neck as the opening; then thrust pins of wood through the lips to hold the mouths closed, finally securing the lips with fiber.

"All the openings must be closed to trap the spirit."

Vasquez glanced at the old Indian. The orange reflection of the flames danced in his eyes, making him look like an underworld demon.

"If the enemy's soul escapes it will be angry and will seek revenge."

"*Si. Comprendo.*" Why was this man telling him this? He only cared about the process, not the superstitious beliefs of savages.

They passed the rest of the night watching the warriors in silence. As dawn of the second day broke, the first rays of sunlight illuminated a younger warrior as he half-filled a large earthenware pot with water, placed it in the fire and squeezed some juice from a vine into it.

When the mixture started boiling, he put a head in and collected rounded stones which he put into the fire. The smell of cooking meat filled the air, reminding Vasquez of his mother's stew. He'd never be able to eat it again.

That afternoon they fished the heads from the pots. They had been shrunk to one third of their original size. The skin looked pale yellow with thick, rubbery consistency. The Indians sewed up the slit in the back, picked up the heated stones with sticks and dropped them into the heads, then rotated them to make the stones roll around inside. A sizzling sound filled the air followed by a smell like burnt leather. Vasquez guzzled more rum to try and dull his senses, but the odor persisted.

As the heads shrank and hardened they used hot sand instead of rocks and smoothed the outer features with smaller rocks. That evening they singed off most of the facial fuzz, except for the eyebrows and eyelashes, then sewed the base of the necks, perforated the crowns, and passed a loop of fiber through them. The finished products were hung from a rack above a fire where they remained all night to be smoked.

Vasquez dozed, waking again at dawn to see the warriors polishing their prizes with pieces of cloth. The smoke had changed the heads from yellow to black. How long had the whole process taken? Too long, Vasquez thought. Too much work. There had to be an easier way.

The men put their trophies around their necks and started off through the forest. Vasquez followed. After a short hike, they came to a hut. One wall faced a steep river bank. A door at each end had been made out of hewn planks.

He felt uncomfortable entering the hut, as if he had stumbled into an intimate moment, so he stayed by the door watching as every man with a shrunken head stuck his spear into the ground, butt down and placed his prize on the point of the spear.

A group of women came in, cut off a chicken's head and drained its blood into a bowl. More women came in with bowls of something black. They painted the right leg of each man in spots with blood and painted black on the left leg. Each man smeared blood on his chest and arms.

The women brought in food and drink while the men danced and brandished their spears. The dance continued all day, ending at dark with much singing and drinking. By this time Vasquez had slipped inside the door. He could tell the Indians were getting drunk so he tried some of their drink. It didn't taste as good as his rum, but it had the same effect.

As the dancers finished, each man wrapped his head in cloth, placed it in an earthenware jar, and either put it over his bed or buried it in the floor of the house. As the celebration waned, Vasquez passed out from drunken exhaustion.

He awoke with a pounding headache and a sick stomach. Except for a few women and children going out the door, the

Jivaros slept soundly. A gourd with some of the native drink lay at his feet. He pushed himself upright with his back to the wall and nursed the gourd until its effects deadened the pounding in his head. He had learned the shrinking process, but didn't know if he could bring himself to use it. Aside from its grisly nature, the length of time and amount of work were too much.

He looked over at the earthenware jars containing heads, then at the fresh burial. Beyond the jars he saw a net containing still more heads and remembered Rodrigo bringing them the bodies. Those heads had to be the counterfeits that Rodrigo sold! Why were they here? Did Rodrigo make them here? No matter.

Vasquez picked up his musket and quickly removed the net full of heads. He emptied two of the earthenware pots of Indian heads into another net and crept out of the hut. Outside he saw the women and children by the river's edge. He hurried off in the opposite direction.

Once he reached the edge of the clearing he started running, but the undergrowth tugged at his ankles causing him to stumble and lose his balance. He fell and the net slipped from his grasp. Shrunken heads rolled and bounced across the jungle floor.

Heart pounding, breath coming in ragged gasps, Vasquez pushed himself up, wiped sweat and dirt from his eyes and grabbed at the scattered heads. When he thought he had them all, he started forward again, then stopped. He'd missed one by the base of a tree. He grabbed it and noticed that the back had split open from the impact. He started to toss it, then on impulse turned it over and saw his daughter's face.

A sob caught in his throat like the tip of a spear and his insides plummeted as if they had been yanked to the ground. He dropped the head, knelt and made the sign of the cross. "Maria," he whispered.

"Papa," she answered. "Why did you lock me in the room?"

He jerked upright. His daughter stood in front of him. His mouth dropped open. His breath wouldn't come. Then he started to shake. "I'm sorry Maria!" He cried. "I didn't mean to hurt you. It was an accident. I had too much to drink."

"But I was sick, papa. I only cried because I was sick. You wouldn't come. Now you have to come with me." She held out her hand.

"No. Leave me alone." He stumbled backward, then heard noises behind him and to the sides.

Shouts filled the air. Then they rushed at him. Something struck him in the head. He felt a sharp pain in his leg. Another in his back. When he went down, they swarmed, slamming his head into the ground and grinding his face in the dirt. Unable to breathe, he turned his head to the side. Maria stood smiling at him.

Someone flipped him onto his back and two others held his arms wide. Another ripped his shirt open. White hot agony shot through him as a spear cut into his chest in a V-shape above his nipples. He writhed and screamed, but only a squeal escaped. Then they peeled his flesh up in a wave of excruciating pain that exposed the lower part of his neck. His bowels let loose. One last gurgled scream was cut short when a spear pierced his neck, ending his pain in a rush of blackness.

*   *   *   *   *

When he came back to consciousness, he heard the Jivaros muted singing from a distance as if it were more of a sensation than an actual sound. Where was he? What happened? Then he remembered the heads. Maria. The agony of the spears flaying his flesh. Was he still sleeping? Had he dreamed it? The pain had gone, but the blackness remained. His eyes, nose, mouth, and ears felt sealed shut and he had no awareness of his body. Rage and fury swept through him as he struggled to free himself, but his attempts were futile.

Vasquez had been trapped in the small dark room of his soul.

DOG GONE

Here, Rusty!"

The lanky Golden Retriever galloped awkwardly across the yard and jumped up on his master. Strings of saliva ran out of the corners of the dog's mouth as he licked Jack's face.

"Atta boy, Rusty. That's my boy." Jack nuzzled the dog's neck and patted his flank. Rusty licked his face again.

Jack's dark-haired girlfriend Nicole watched Jack and Rusty. She felt warmth for Jack, his muscular frame, shaggy blond hair and beard. She loved his boyish innocence, puppy-dog eyes, flannel shirts, and hiking boots. A tiny smile formed on her lips, then she saw the dog slobbering. Her smile faded.

She hated the dog. Rusty was always there, snuggling into bed, sitting on the couch, going with them to the beach, visiting. Everywhere they went, Rusty with his fleas, slobber, shit and shedding went with them.

Even when he wasn't there, he was. His hairs, his smell. That *dog* smell. Everywhere. Gross. And if there weren't physical reminders, there were mental.

"Nicole," Jack would say. "Rusty sat up today. He fetched the stick. I took him to the vet. He was so cute." He did this.

He did that.

She didn't think she could take anymore, yet day after day she tolerated the dog. She knew if she stuck it out, sooner or later she might have Jack all to herself — without his slobbering mutt.

She looked at her watch. If they didn't get going, they'd be late again. She slid open the glass door that led to the back yard. "Jack, honey," she called, "we'd better leave right now or we'll miss the show."

Jack and the dog both looked over. Rusty jumped down and bounded toward the door. Nicole slammed it. The dog leaped up against it, a slap of mud, paws, saliva and wet nose smearing the glass. Gross.

She could hear Jack's laugh through the glass. "Come on, babe. Rusty wants to play with you. You know how much he likes you. Come on out. Just for a minute."

She shook her head and pointed at her watch. No way in hell would she let that smelly mutt ruin her new sweater. She turned from the door, listening to Jack soothing the dog.

"That's my boy."

The dog whined.

"Sorry, buddy. Nicole doesn't want to play, but I'll be back later. We'll go for a walk. Play catch."

While Jack changed his shirt, Nicole had the feeling of being watched. She looked out the window and saw Rusty staring at her. When their eyes met, the dog growled.

He stopped as soon as Jack came out of the bedroom. His tail wagged. Jack smiled and shook his head. "Isn't he cute?"

After a Mel Gibson movie, they enjoyed a late Italian dinner in a candlelit corner of Sorrentinos. Jack had eggplant parmigiana, Nicole fettucine primavera. They held hands while they talked. Warm feelings and tender words softly spoken in the subdued glow of the candle. The mood went with them back to Jack's where their lovemaking bloomed full and passionate as they shared loving caresses and intimate words whispered afterward in their gentle embrace. Soft skin touching soft skin.

When Jack started to get up Nicole held him tighter. "Don't leave, honey. Stay with me."

"I'll be right back."

Reluctantly, she let him go and lay on her back, still savoring thoughts of Jack inside her. She heard noises in the hall and smiled. Good, she thought, that didn't take long.

A moment later she felt paws digging into her thighs through the blanket. Rusty was on her, his hot, moist, dog breath in her face. A cold, wet nose, then a slimy tongue lapped her cheek.

"Get him off of me, Jack!" She pushed Rusty off her chest. The dog jumped again, his snout burrowing into her crotch. She squealed and pushed him away.

Jack came in a moment later. "Down, Rusty!" he commanded.

Rusty cowered on the floor. Jack took him by the collar and led him away. "It's okay, buddy," he said softly. "She's a little upset. You surprised her, that's all." He pushed the dog out of the room and closed the door, turning his back on the scratching and whining to face Nicole. She saw the hurt in his eyes. "Sorry, babe. He's a big dog, but he's also a big baby. He's used to sleeping with me. He doesn't know any better."

She wiped her face with the sheet and glared at him. The dog whimpered and clawed at the door.

Jack slipped under the covers and cuddled her. She stiffened, resisting his touch, then gave in to his caresses. Rusty grew quiet as they kissed. They made love again and fell asleep in each other's arms.

The sound of whimpers awoke her. She looked over at the other side of the bed. Jack was gone. She heard his voice out in the hall. "It's okay, Rusty. That's my boy. Sorry, buddy, she's not used to you yet. What's that? No, no. Of course I love you best." The crying stopped. She lay awake waiting for Jack to return. When he didn't, she rolled over and went back to sleep.

She awoke in the morning with something warm and heavy covering her legs. She opened her eyes and saw Rusty asleep at the foot of the bed. Jack slept beside her. She wanted to push the dog off, but the sight of Jack sleeping peacefully made her decide to wait and discuss it with him when he woke.

Things had gotten out of hand.

She remembered the morning she awoke with her hand under her pillow, touching something hard and cold with funny textures. A bone with dried, stringy gristle hanging off the end of it. Another time she woke to find a sticky chew-toy dropped beside her face. And the dog hairs. Everywhere. And the dog smells. It drove her crazy.

She lay stiff, glaring at the dog, waiting for Jack to stir, her anger seething. Rusty popped open one eye as if he knew she watched him, then opened the other. His big eyes seemed to plead. He lifted his head and let his mouth drop into that big, dumb "dog smile" as Jack called it. Saliva flowed.

She pulled her legs up and pushed him off the bed. Rusty hit the floor with a thump. Jack awoke. She watched as the dog sidled up to him and licked his hand.

Disgusting.

"Jack, I can't go on like this," she said. "I can't take him anymore."

He scratched Rusty behind the ear. "What's wrong with him?"

She snorted. "Nothing. It's us. Our relationship." She sat up and leaned against the headboard, arms crossed. She felt her mouth turning down at the corners.

Jack sat up, wiped the sleep from his eyes and stared at her, a half-puzzled, half-hurt expression stealing across his face. "What's Rusty got to do with our relationship?"

"Everything," she blurted. "He's always with us. In bed, on the couch, on the floor. We don't get any time alone. He's always there, damn it." She bit her lower lip. "I feel like I'm competing with him."

He frowned and grew quiet for a moment, then burst into laughter.

"What's so funny?" she said. Her eyes burned.

He grabbed his stomach. "You," he said between chortles. "I can't believe it. You're jealous of a dog!"

His words hit hard. Her face felt hot as though she'd been slapped. She wiped a tear away. "Even when we're alone, he's there. Rusty this, Rusty that. Rusty took a shit today. Rusty rolled over. Rusty chased a ball. Rusty. Rusty. Rusty. I'm sick of it. What about me?"

"I'm sorry, babe." He reached for her and she pulled back.

Jack ruffled the dog's head. Rusty's mouth opened into his "dog grin." "I thought you understood. Rusty's my buddy. It's like we're — connected or something."

"If you're so close," she snapped, "where does that leave me?

You mean to tell me you feel closer to your dog than to me?"

He shook his head and smiled. For a second his smile resembled Rusty's dog smile. Geez, she thought. He's even starting to look like his mutt.

"No. No, that's not it." He shot Rusty a sideways glance, then lowered his voice. "I just want us all to be together. Like a family." He leaned over and took her in his arms. "You know I love you, babe."

His breath on her neck aroused her.

"I'm sorry, honey," she whispered.

His tongue darted into her ear.

"I didn't mean to make a scene. I don't want to compete. It's just that I love you. You know that, don't you?"

"I know, babe."

Nicole held him tighter and peered over his shoulder. Rusty sat at the foot of the bed studying them with his head tilted sideways, looking perplexed.

That's right you fucking mutt, she thought. *I'm* number one. Not you. She glared, rubbed Jack's back with her left hand and gave Rusty the finger with her right.

After she and Jack made love, she got dressed. When she went to put on her shoes, dampness crept through her hose into her sock. She screamed in frustration.

Rusty had pissed in her shoe.

Jack's birthday came that weekend. Nicole wanted to make it special. She left work early on Friday and spent her whole paycheck, even postponing the purchase of a few necessities so she could buy Jack a leather jacket. She wrapped the box in blue and green pastel tissue and put it on his kitchen table with a card.

She took him out for Thai food, promising him he could open his present when they returned.

After drinks and dancing they returned to the darkened house. Jack flipped on the light and Nicole let out a startled scream.

Blue and green pastel tissue and torn bits of cardboard lay shredded all over the floor. Jack's new jacket lay in the center of the mess, chewed and tattered. Nicole caught the flash of a tail disappearing around the corner.

She threw her purse at the dog and chased him through the house until Jack grabbed her and let the dog escape. She broke down sobbing.

Jack took her in his arms and hugged her. She looked up from his shoulder and saw Rusty peering around the corner. She started trembling. Jack glanced back, then went for the dog. "C'mere Rusty." He grabbed the dog by the collar. "Bad dog!" He thumped him on the snout.

Dragging him to the center of the room, he rubbed his nose in the remains of the jacket. "Bad dog!" Rusty whined and looked up at Nicole with sad looking eyes. Jack dragged him back outside. "You can sleep out here tonight." He came back in and cuddled Nicole against his chest. "I'm sorry, hon. I don't know what got into him."

They ended up in the bedroom where they made love before falling asleep. Nicole woke up in the middle of the night and found Jack gone. Sitting up, she eased the bedroom window open. She could hear Jack talking to his dog in the yard.

"Don't be mad at me, buddy," he pleaded. "I had to do it. What's that? Oh. She doesn't mean to hurt your feelings. She's a girl. You know how they are."

The phone rang the next day. Jack picked it up and talked for awhile, concern showing on his face.

"I'm sorry, babe," he said after hanging up. "My dad had a bad fall."

"Is he all right?"

"He's going to be fine, but my mother needs help."

Nicole felt her heart sink. "How long will you be gone?"

"Three, four days. Five at the most.

She wrapped her arms around his waist and hugged him. "I'm going to miss you. Can I give you a ride to the airport?"

Jack kissed her on the forehead. "I was hoping." He held her at arm's length and peered into her eyes. "I hate to ask, but I've got one more favor...."

"Rusty."

"I know how much you hate the smell, but if you could stop by once a day and make sure he's got food and water..." He paused. "It would mean a lot to me."

Nicole spied a scrap of pastel tissue sticking out of the wastebasket. "Okay, hon, but I will *not* babysit him and I will *not* play with him. I'll stop by and feed him for *you. Not* for him."

Jack pulled her close. "Thanks, honey."

She took him to the airport that afternoon. On the way home she stopped at the grocery store and bought two large cans of dog food, a small steak, and a large package of rat poison. She went to Jack's and led Rusty out to the backyard, all the while talking to him and patting him.

"Thatta boy, Rusty," she said in her best baby talk. "Come with Mama. Are you hungry?"

Rusty looked up at her, tail wagging, tongue lolling. She

picked up his bowls from the yard and brought them inside holding them at arm's length. The dog whined.

"I'll teach you to fuck with me, you stupid mutt," she said sweetly. She scratched him behind the ear. "I'm going to fix a *special* treat for you."

She diced the steak and fried it, then mixed it and the grease with a can of dog food. She threw in some spices and a large dose of poison. Sniffing the concoction, she smiled. "Smells good to me. That's right, Rusty boy." She brought the steaming mixture and a bowl of water out to the yard. "This will taste better than the jacket."

Rusty poked his snout into the mixture and gobbled. While he emptied the bowls she went back to the house and got a chair só she could watch Rusty from behind the glass door. When he finished eating, he lay down and took a nap.

She waited.

An hour later he stood on wobbly legs and vomited a thick green mixture of blood, bile, and the remains of his meal. Nicole stared, horrified as he looked up at her. His eyes seemed accusing.

He staggered toward her. Halfway, his legs gave out and he collapsed. His bowels let loose. Nicole put her face in her hands. Rusty screeched, his cries sounding like that of a human baby. He whined and crawled closer, finally dropping in front of the glass door. She lowered her hands.

He gazed up at her with a wild, unfocused look.

His tongue lolled out of his mouth. He whimpered and his breathing came in short, labored pants. His head lay flat against the ground, one eye staring up at Nicole. A puddle of urine spread out beneath him, his body jerked and his "dog smile" filled his face. A moment later, he stopped breathing.

Nicole lined a trash can with three Hefty lawn and leaf bags and pushed Rusty's limp carcass into it with a shovel. When she got most of his bulk in, she held her breath and tipped the can upright. Rusty's limp form slid sideways. His tongue dangled from his open mouth. Vacant eyes stared up at her. She quickly tied the bags, put the lid on the can and dragged it to her car.

Back in the yard, she hosed away Rusty's mess, then drove out of town. She buried the dog and the empty poison containers in a shallow grave a few hundred feet from the side of the road. Exhausted, she drove home and collapsed into bed without taking her clothes off.

She awoke the following morning to the ringing of the phone.

"Hello?"

"Nicole, this is Jack."

Her heart rose in her throat. "Oh — hi, hon."

"How's Rusty? I'm worried about him. Did you check on him last night?"

"Oh, Jack." Her voice trembled on the verge of tears. She didn't like the feeling but knew it would help her sound more convincing. "I've been out all night. Rusty's gone. Somebody must have stolen him." Hot tears fell on her arm as she cradled the phone.

"Gone? Stolen? Did you call the cops?"

"Not yet. I was going to go out looking again today."

"Call the cops." Jack's voice sounded strange, like a terrified child. She had never heard him sound like that
before.

"Of course. I'm — I'm so sorry. I don't know what to say."

She sobbed. "I'm so sorry." She meant it.

Except for his breathing, the line stayed silent for an uncomfortably long time. Then she heard Jack's voice, barely a whisper. "It's all right, hon. It's not your fault."

She met him at the airport three nights later. His face looked hollow, his eyes sunken with dark rings underneath. His features were gaunt as though he'd aged twenty years in a few days. He moved in a stupor.

Nicole ran to him. "Honey, are you all right? Are you sick?"

"I'm okay," he mumbled. "Just a little run down."

"You look like hell. You need some rest, babe. Something to eat."

He looked at her, head moving slowly, face twisting in pain. "I need Rusty," he whispered.

She fought back a rising sob, took him in her arms and gently stroked the back of his head. She could feel him shaking. "Come on, honey. I'll take you home."

Nicole drove to Jack's and cooked him dinner. He only ate a few bites before pushing his plate away. "Can't eat," he muttered.

She cleared the table and started washing their dishes. When she turned to talk to him, Jack had gone. She found him sitting cross-legged in the back yard, Rusty's chew-toy pressed to his nose. She backed away from the door, went to the kitchen and finished the dishes. Jack came in half an hour later and went straight to bed. Nicole climbed in after him.

He tensed when she put her hand on his shoulder, so she left him alone. He fell asleep quickly. She studied him, wondering how long he would stay like this. She knew how much he loved the dog, but things had gone a little too far. For the first time in their relationship, she worried about Jack's mental health. Was he losing it? She lay awake a long time before rolling over onto her side and dozing.

Rusty whined in the darkness. Damn him. He'd gotten into the room again — she caught herself. Rusty's gone. She sat up in bed, eyes wide. The sound came from beside her. She looked at Jack, asleep, whining like a dog. Like Rusty. The sound frightened her. She didn't know whether to wake him or leave him alone.

She leaned over and stroked his head. The cries softened to a whimper, then into shallow breathing. She took a deep breath, lay down and went back to sleep.

She awoke first the next morning and rolled over to watch him. Her breath caught in her throat. Rusty's chew-toy lay next to Jack's head. She reached over and touched it.

Wet.

Repulsed, she slipped out of bed without waking Jack, showered, and went to work with the uneasy feeling that Jack was slipping away from her. She decided that if his strange behavior continued, she'd call a doctor — see about getting him into therapy.

After work, she stopped for groceries and went to Jack's. She found him curled up on the couch surrounded by dog toys, Rusty's blanket clutched close to his face.

She set the groceries down and sat next to him on the couch. "Maybe we'd better get help. I know how much you loved Rusty, Jack, but don't you think it's time to let him go?"

"Rusty's still here." He pointed to his head. "With me."

She fought back rising impatience. "Jack, this has gone too far. Tomorrow I'm going to call a doctor."

Jack stared back at her, but didn't answer.

As soon as she crawled into bed that night, she smelled Rusty as if he'd just been there. A chill scrambled across her scalp. There were dog hairs everywhere. Funny, she hadn't noticed them the other night. Must've been too tired. When she slid beneath the sheets her foot hit something small and hard. She reached down and pulled out a gristle covered bone.

She wanted to make love to Jack, but he was acting so strange, distant. She decided to wait. Pulling the covers up, she fell into an uneasy sleep and slipped down into an uncomfortable dream.

Rusty jumped onto the bed, claws digging into her legs, his nose burrowing into her crotch. Gross. She swatted at him. He crawled up on her, tongue hanging, saliva oozing from his mouth. She tried to push him off and he growled.

Startled, she opened her eyes and saw Jack leaning over her, smiling his silly, doglike smile. She let out a squeal. "Oh, honey. You scared me."

Jack pressed his face into the curve of her neck and licked her. Goosebumps prickled over her body.

When she woke the following morning, she had scratches on her legs.

Two nights later she lay awake wanting to reach over and embrace Jack. She propped her head on one arm and studied his sleeping form. Should she wake him? No, better wait, they could make love in the morning. She closed her eyes and drifted.

The sound of growling came to her.

A moment later the dark, shaggy- headed form leaped up on the bed. The smell. It lunged at her, hot animal breath moist on her face, stringy saliva covering her neck.

She looked into the eyes of her attacker a moment before she felt pressure on her throat; then she opened her mouth to scream. Teeth tore into her neck, ripping through her windpipe, choking off her voice. She watched her own bright, arterial blood spurt onto the sheets, then she stared into Jack's eyes and wondered.

Rusty?

MIND GAMES

John Schmitten glanced at the clock at five minutes 'til five and breathed a sigh of relief. He planned on leaving the office in peace until his boss, George Hoffman, came in. "Do you have those proposals?"

"First thing in the morning."

The heavy, bearded man gazed at John from behind thick glasses, studying him in his own weird version of scrutiny — looking at him, but not looking at him as if John were an insect under a microscope.

"We need them tomorrow. If we lose this account...."

"Don't worry, they'll be done." John snapped his briefcase shut and walked out, leaving Hoffman behind.

John sat at home that night, Axl his cat in his lap, a beer in his hand and a bottle of Jack Daniels in front of him. "Hoffman's such an asshole." He stroked the cat. "Master of all browbeaters. What I wouldn't do to free myself from him."

He glanced around the room — bare except for a black and white T.V. and small radio. "Alimony," he muttered. "How can I even meet someone living in a shithole like this. Cindy takes all my money." He drained his beer and poured a shot of Jack Daniels.

"What can I do, Axl? Between Hoffman and Cindy I have no life."

He spied the paper at his feet and flipped through it, stopping at the personals section. An ad jumped out at him.

LOST IN A DEAD END JOB? BORED? LONELY? WANT TO MEET MEMBERS OF THE OPPOSITE SEX? MAKE NEW FRIENDS? DO YOU WANT TO FREE YOURSELF FROM A MINDLESS EXISTENCE FOREVER? IF YOU ANSWERED YES TO THE PRECEDING QUESTIONS, DIAL 1-900-FREEDOM. NO FEE!

"Lonely hearts club." He tossed the paper aside and drained another shot of Jack. Axl purred.

Three shots later he picked up the paper and read the ad again. Two more shots and he was dialing the phone. "What the hell, I've got nothing to lose."

Two rings and a sexy pre-recorded female voice came on the line. "Want your desires fulfilled? Meet some members of the opposite sex? Come play with us. State your desires at the beep, then leave your name and number."

John felt a surge of giddiness when he gave his number, then a flush of anger. "It's real simple. I want to free myself from Hoffman, my ex-wife, alimony, and all the pressures of my stupid life, then I want to meet a beautiful girl who can give me better company than my damn cat." He slammed the receiver down and Axl jumped.

On impulse he redialed and heard another recorded female voice. This one not so sexy. "The number you have reached has been disconnected and is no longer in service. If you feel you have reached this number in error..."

He hung up and tried again several times, but got the same results.

A couple of weeks passed. Hoffman kept John miserable with his constant pressure for new proposals, while Cindy clamored for more money. Work got busier and they hired more employees, one of them a new guy for the art department.

Aleister Blackwood wore one of those silly pentagrams that hung from a gold chain. He sported a pointed goatee, arching eyebrows, and a nose that seemed a little too long. Wispy strands of honey-colored hair lay across a bald spot on top of his head. Short, heavy-set, and meticulously groomed, he always wore black. John suspected he had six more identical turtle neck outfits hanging in his closet. His nails were manicured but not quite pointed, except for the little fingernail on his left hand which he painted gloss black, offsetting a pinkie ring with a blood red ruby. To top it all off, he had one gold earring.

An upside down cross.

John's first instincts were to steer clear and let the loony-tune stay in la-la land, but he kept running into Aleister in the copy room, the lunch room and the men's room. Their meetings seemed more than accidental — as if the dude knew where John would be. Whenever their paths crossed it made John uneasy. It wasn't so much the way Aleister looked or anything he said. It was the way his dark eyes probed John. Hoffman scrutinized him the same way: the way his cat looked at a mouse before ripping it apart.

John did his best to avoid the new guy until he sensed Aleister behind him in the lunchroom one day. His spine crawled as he imagined Aleister's gaze on the back of his head. The awkward silence grew into an almost palpable pressure for John to say something. When it grew unbearable, he spun around.

Aleister's eyes flashed, taking in John, then his usually unexpressive face brightened and he smiled with what John's mother called a Cheshire cat smile. John called it a shit-eating grin. "Hoffman's really on your ass, isn't he?"

Aleister's directness caught John off guard. "Hoffman's on everybody's ass."

Aleister nodded. "But you're a pretty cool customer." His eyes brightened. "Want to go have a beer after work? I'll buy."

"Thanks, but I can't. Hoffman's crawling up my ass for his damn proposals."

Aleister's eyes dimmed. "I'll take a rain check."

He bounced into John's cubicle the next morning. "I'm having a party on Saturday the twenty-third."

"I'm not sure..."

"You and I both know you have nothing happening. I won't take no for an answer. It'll give you a chance to make new friends. Meet some members of the opposite sex." He wiggled his eyebrows. "Guaranteed to free you from loneliness and a mindless existence."

Where have I heard that before? John thought. "What time and where?"

He heard the music from the street. Loud, head-banging, heavy metal. He took the apartment steps two at a time, anxious to see what kind of crowd Aleister hung out with.

Aleister greeted him at the door, a thick wave of incense-laced marijuana smoke floating out behind him. Candles flickered in the background giving the impression of a pagan cave. John could barely make out the dark outlines of people crowding the room. "John, my man." Aleister pulled him into the apartment. "Glad you came, I was getting worried. Wouldn't be a party without you."

The music stopped. In the sudden silence, everyone trained their eyes on John, then the first bars of Three Dog Night's "Mama Told Me Not To Come" filled the apartment. A girl giggled in another room, and everyone went back to their conversations.

Aleister pressed a cold Heineken into John's hand. "Drink up and mingle. I have to check on something. Back in a few."

Smoky haze hung thick in the air, punctuated by soft halos of dancing candlelight. John found himself drawn to the darkness and had the feeling of being watched. Turning, he locked eyes with a gorgeous fox in tight jeans and an even tighter spandex top that barely contained a set of grapefruit-sized breasts. Straight blonde hair flowed over her shoulders, cascading all the way down her back. She smiled, batted her eyelashes and nudged the girl beside her who could have been her twin, except that her hair was raven black. He couldn't believe his eyes. Two beauties. Nice curves, dark eyes, and red, red lips. Flawless white teeth.

"Hi, my name's John." He stepped toward them.

"You're the guy from Aleister's work." The blonde smiled and took a hit off a joint someone handed her, then passed it to John.

He took a deep drag and held it in, letting its narcotic effect slide over his brain like a shroud. It had a bitter aftertaste which he washed away with beer.

When she turned to whisper something to her friend, John marveled at their two perfect forms in profile. Delicate shoulders, perfect breasts, and graceful arching backs that sloped down into two awesome behinds.

They both looked at John, smiled at each other and giggled, charming him all the more. Someone passed him another joint. The second hit sank over his brain like a velvet hammer. He shook his head. "Pretty good stuff." He'd never smoked anything this strong — or bitter. He drained his beer, but the taste lingered.

The black-haired girl winked, then Aleister appeared at his side, handing him another cold Heineken.

"Interesting group of friends you have." The buzz in John's head made the words emerge before his brain could catch up. "I can't figure you."

"Figure me?"

"You know — black clothes, pentagram, and all that shit."

Aleister laughed and the twins giggled, then he leaned closer until John felt his breath in his ear. "Shit, John, it's all a game."

"Game? I dont..." Someone turned the music down. John stared at the beer in his hand. His vision blurred.

"You know," the blonde girl said. "Your desires fulfilled. Meet members of the opposite sex?" She winked. "Come play with us."

He recognized the voice.

Aleister slapped him between the shoulders, jolting him back to the moment. "Drink up, partner, it's time for you to learn."

Game? John looked at the girls while they studied him, then realized that the rest of the party conversations had ceased. He glanced around. People drifted in from the other rooms, all converging on Aleister, as if the word "game" had been the signal they'd been waiting for. His throat felt tight. "What do you mean, learn?"

Everyone directed their attention to Aleister. "Ever hear of role-playing games?"

"Like that Dungeons and Dragons shit?"

Aleister beamed. "Along those lines, only much more sophisticated." A squat, pimple-faced man with dark hair hanging down one side of his face emerged from a back room carrying a large black five-sided box which he placed at Aleister's feet.

John had a strong urge to leave, but the pressure of everyone watching him kept him immobile. "I don't know. I've never done anything like this. I doubt I'd be any good."

"You're perfect," said the blonde. She glanced sideways at her twin, who said, "I'd play with him any day."

John studied the expectant faces and the thought crossed his mind that he couldn't leave, even if he wanted to.

Aleister held out his hand. The two girls placed theirs in his and he kissed their slender fingers. "I hold in my hand, Flora and Fauna, spirits of mother earth and fertility — the receptacles of the fires of passion which stir within us all."

A pleasant tingle danced across John's groin then his thoughts grew fuzzy, as if someone had wrapped them in gauze.

Aleister released the girls and spun toward a wan and lanky blond man with light blue eyes. "And here we have Stratus, a spirit of the air."

John glanced from Aleister to Stratus and bit back a laugh. Next he's gonna introduce Dopey and Sneezy.

"And then there's Crystal, a child of the water." A short,

full bodied girl, with flowing dark hair and deep green eyes stepped to the front of the crowd.

"Okay," John said, humoring Aleister and his friends. "I get it. Earth, air, and water. What about fire?"

Aleister crossed his arms and smiled. The light through his hair reflected red highlights John had never noticed before. "I am the fire of baptism and purification."

John's throat felt stuffed with cotton. He took a long drink of his beer and tried to think of an excuse to leave, but one look at Aleister's friends resigned him to the fact that he'd never get out.

Aleister's hands danced through the air like hummingbirds and everyone took a seat on the floor. Aleister, John, Flora, and Fauna sat in the inner circle, the five-sided box at the very center. Aleister removed the lid and took out a bell, tarot cards, an old, leather bound book, a silver chalice, a pair of five-sided dice with numbers instead of dots, black candles, and a black silk hooded robe. The dark-haired man in the leather vest took the candles, put them in silver holders and placed them at five points around the circle. No one made a sound.

John suddenly felt cold. "What the hell kind of game is this?"

Flora and Fauna smiled in unison, dreamy-eyed expressions filling their faces. "A game of desire," Flora said.

"And passion," Fauna added, directing her smile at John.

Aleister donned the robe and pulled the hood over his head obscuring his face. He shuffled the tarot cards and made a series of elaborate gestures over the deck. Flora and Fauna each drew a card: Flora, The High Priestess; Fauna, The Five Of Swords. Aleister bowed and presented the deck to John.

John reached into the middle and drew The Fool.

Flora and Fauna knelt on each side of him. Fauna took his hand and placed it between hers and Flora's. Aleister picked up the book and stood over them. Flora and Fauna placed John's other hand on top of it.

This is too weird, John thought.

"Do you solemnly swear with your heart, freely giving your soul as hostage, to abide by the rules of the alternate universe you are about to enter?" Aleister asked.

John tried peering up under the hood to see Aleister's expression, but the folds of silk obscured his features. Something told him to leave. He looked at the upturned faces of the two beautiful girls flanking him. Something else told him to stay.

"Sure, Aleister. I swear."

"Good!" Aleister threw back his hood and laughed. Flora and Fauna each kissed John and the other people in the room started talking again.

John sighed with relief.

"You've attained the status of acolyte," Aleister said. "Now we can get the game underway."

"I thought we already had."

"You've earned the right to put your fate with the dice." He held them in his palm. "Since you're new, you get to roll first."

John took the dice and tossed them.

"Thirteen." Aleister reached into the box, withdrew a five-sided card and set it in front of John. "Study it," he said. "It's a mandala. Let it take you to another place."

John stared at the pattern: an overblown gordian knot that wrapped in on itself and focused his attention toward its center. The twisted lines writhed as if they had a life of their own, circling both clockwise and counterclockwise, drawing him into the figure.

The people around him began to sing, their voices punctuated by the peals of a bell. John found himself listening to their voices, sometimes harmonizing, sometimes eddying off on their own tangents. The sounds caressed his senses, their totality taking on a rhythm of their own. In and out.

Breathing.

A heartbeat.

Pulsing back and forth. Clockwise and counterclockwise.

In unison with the mandala.

A rush of color and sound flooded through him. He forced his eyes from the pattern, locking his gaze on Flora and Fauna. His perceptions shifted toward a deeper, more meaningful poignancy. The singing sounded clearer. The features of the two girls looked more beautiful than ever. The gentle rise of their cheekbones, the graceful curves of their bodies and their lithe movements. Two sets· of eyes sparkled in the soft candlelight. Earrings glinted gold. He became aware of their perfume washing over him. He didn't recognize the scent, only its effect which focused all his senses to a peak, at the center of which stood the two girls — the nimbus of his desires.

What the hell was going on?

He tried to voice his thoughts, but the words came out jumbled, his mind racing, mouth lagging. He looked from the girls to Aleister and back again. All three smiled as if everything were normal.

Another shift and his thoughts came quicker. Disjointed, yet more intense. Broken flashes flickering like an old black and white movie. Alternating.

Coherence.

Incoherence.

Flora and Fauna. Undressed. Beside him. Soft kisses. His shirt, pants. Gone. The two women flowed over him in an overwhelming caress of tender touches and wet kisses. Delicate wings of ecstasy fluttered through him as his body gave itself over to their ministrations.

A curtain drew back on a wall revealing a low table. Above it hung an inverted triangle: at it's center an upside-down cross. The girls whispered unintelligibly in each ear, not words, but emotions.

Bliss.

Aleister's voice droned on in the background. The soft touch of Flora and Fauna's bare breasts on John's skin gave him goose bumps and an erection which embarrassed him.

Hands lifted and carried him to the altar. Aleister read from the black book while Flora and Fauna pleasured John. Exultation engulfed him as the inner circle of participants placed their hands on him. He jumped at a pinprick on his finger, then someone squeezed a few drops of his blood into a chalice and mixed it with wine. All the participants drank, giving John the last sip.

Flora and Fauna made love to him, first one, then the other, then both, every part of him finding every part of them until he couldn't make a distinction. Intertwined with their essences he sensed Aleister as if he were a partner in the sex act, living through and with the girls as part of the same presence. The thought of sex with another male sent a cold bolt of revulsion flashing through him, but not before his consuming passion darted through him, toppling him over the edge. He shuddered at the rush of his climax, helpless as its ripples of poignancy carried him down into the blackness....

He felt warm darkness press down on his chest like a spectral hand, then a mournful cry. He opened his eyes. Two yellow orbs peered back at him from the recesses of a black furry head. A gaping jaw opened, revealing needlelike teeth.

"Hey, Axl, buddy." His voice sounded as if he were talking through a mouthful of straw. The cat purred and nuzzled his face.

John sat up in bed, not knowing how he got there. His head felt swollen, his body depleted as if something had drained him of energy. He tried to remember how he'd arrived home, but drew a blank. His only memory of the previous night came to him in a collage of jagged images.

Aleister's party. Two beautiful women. Had he drunk too much? Smoked too much pot? They'd played some kind of bizarre game. He flashed on a blur of tarot cards, dice, and black candles. Then the girls — had they?

He had a lingering feeling of violation. Used, then discarded. No way two beers and a couple of hits off a joint could do that to him. Had to be something....

Aleister must have slipped him L.S.D. in his beer! Nothing else could explain his distorted memories. A rush of anger flooded through him. Son-of-a-bitch. Wait 'til he got his hands on that little bastard.

When he awoke on Monday, his body felt weak and feverish as if fighting an infection, but when he thought about confronting Aleister, his anger drove him out of bed.

He breezed past the receptionist and pushed his way through

the doors to the art department where he found Aleister's area. Vacant.

He stormed back to the front. "Where the hell is he?"

She looked up startled, her big brown eyes blinking. "Who?"

"Aleister from the art department."

"There's no Aleister in the art department."

"What is this, some kind of joke?"

Her puzzled expression told him it wasn't.

Ten minutes later, he ran up the stairs to Aleister's and peered through a curtainless window at empty rooms. He slammed his hand against the wall. "Shit!" Putting his forearm against the door, he leaned forward, resting his head in the crook of his arm. Something glinted from beneath the door. He reached down and withdrew a tiny gold inverted cross earring.

He decided to go home, relax and get back his strength. Halfway to his car he spotted two sets of gorgeous legs strutting up the street side by side: two provocatively swaying asses in two sets of short shorts. Two flowing manes, one raven, the other platinum.

Flora and Fauna.

He'd know their movements anywhere. He ran after them, grabbed Flora by the shoulder and spun her around. She smiled seductively and ran her tongue slowly over her upper lip.

"Time to play," Fauna giggled behind him.

He looked over his shoulder.

"You're in the game now," Flora said.

He turned back and a blast of vomit-smelling breath hit him in the face, then she shrieked like something half-human. John blinked and stared dumbfounded at a gap-toothed lady with greasy, tangled hair. She wore a ragged coat and clutched a tattered Hefty bag to her chest, eyes wide with terror. He heard another scream behind him, then something hit him on the side of the head.

He staggered sideways, trying to fathom his confusion. Two shopping carts. How could he have missed them? A second bag lady, short and squat with a stained windbreaker and eyes wild with rage, swung an aluminum cane at him. He ducked and stumbled backward toward his car then drove away quickly so no one could see him.

He found Axl waiting for him at his apartment. "Hey, pal, you won't believe what I just saw."

The cat stared at him as if waiting to hear.

John spent the rest of the day in bed, drifting in and out of consciousness, the exotic images of Flora and Fauna mixing with the hideous features of the two bag ladies. Axl stayed curled at his feet.

He forced himself to go to work the next day. Monday's absence had put him behind. His phone didn't stop ringing and Hoffman badgered him for overdue reports. He thought he glimpsed Aleister in the parking lot, but when he went out to investigate, he realized he'd been mistaken.

Hoffman appeared at ten minutes 'til five. "Where are they?," he said. "The board of directors are anxious to see you do well in the game."

"Huh?" John looked at Hoffman and saw a lanky blond man with pastel blue eyes. Aleister's friend, Stratus. Remembering his encounter with the bag ladies, John stifled the urge to lash out. "Game? What game? You never told me the rules."

"Find your way through the maze," Stratus said. "Now that you've reached the second level, the stakes are higher."

John rubbed his eyes. "What do you mean, higher? What are you talking about?"

Hoffman frowned. "Have you listened to anything I've said?"

"Sorry. I'll have the proposals tomorrow."

Hoffman continued staring, then rose and walked out without another word.

The next morning John saw a girl with long, flowing dark hair and green eyes wearing a low cut satin blouse at the receptionist's desk. His chest tightened. Crystal from Aleister's party. "What the hell are you doing to me?"

The receptionist looked up from her work. "What are you talking about, John? Are you all right? You look like you've seen a ghost."

Over the next few days the "sightings" grew in frequency. He couldn't catch up with his work and he couldn't get a decent night's sleep without waking up in a cold sweat.

More and more people came to his desk, demanding things. More often than not, they'd change before his eyes. Sometimes, they'd make obscure references to the game in the middle of normal conversations, other times they'd take on the mannerisms of Aleister or one of his friends. People on the street shouted at him, telling him of his progress in the game. The checkout girl at the grocery store changed from Flora to Fauna to Crystal back to Aleister, all giving him conflicting pieces of information about the game. Her features never changed, only her voice and mannerisms as if she were a stand-up comedian doing impersonations.

Sometimes Hoffman came in as Aleister. Other times a co-worker acted like another player who cryptically told John to meet him at a certain address. John would go and discover a dead end street, the last number one digit short of the address. He felt increasingly frustrated. They all seemed to be playing the same "game," but he didn't know the rules. Didn't know how to play.

The combination of lost sleep and constant antagonism wore John down. He had all he could do to keep from attacking his "adversaries."

After a traffic cop stopped him and told him to find a secret passage and look for a hidden map, John hurried home and locked the door behind him. Axl strutted out of the kitchen, tail and head held high. "Hey, Axl, buddy." John patted him with a shaking hand. "I'm losing it."

Axl turned his head sideways and opened his mouth as if yawning. "Don't let those assholes get you down, partner." His sing-song voice sounded high-pitched like an articulated meow.

John's heart jerked as if hooked by a fisherman's gaff. He put his hands to his face and slid to the floor. "Not you," he whispered.

Axl hopped up onto his lap and sat back on his haunches. "Why not me? You need somebody on your side."

John shook his head.

"All the others are against you." Axl licked the fur on his foreleg. "That dipshit Aleister and his gang of weirdos are playing games with your mind, man. You need to get things straight. Listen to me, I'll tell you what to do."

"How do I know I can trust you?"

"Come on man, get real. I owe you. You've been feeding me all these years. If I let anything happen to you, I don't eat. Some fool will put me in a shelter and I'll probably get the gas chamber."

John stared at his cat. The more he pondered it, the more Axl made sense. "Okay, dude." John stroked Axl's head. " How can I make things right?"

"I know how to make all this shit cease and desist."

"I'm all ears."

John walked into work swinging his briefcase, its reassuring weight helping him feel confident for the first time in weeks. The usual receptionist, not Flora, Fauna or Crystal smiled at him from the front desk. A good sign.

He went to his desk, set his briefcase in front of him and waited. A few minutes later, Hoffman stepped into his office. "You'd better have those proposals," he said. "The board's meeting in two hours." Beady eyes blinked from behind thick glasses, then Aleister winked.

"Got it all right here." John smiled and patted his briefcase, then crossed his arms.

Hoffman's eyes bulged. His face reddened. "So what are you waiting for? Let's have them." Aleister giggled.

"Now?"

"Now!"

John opened the briefcase, pulled out a .357 and leveled it at Hoffman. The old man's eyes looked like silver dollars behind his glasses, then John squeezed off two shots, sending Hoffman's blood and brains splattering across the cubicle. Hoffman stood staring, open-mouthed before collapsing to the floor. Blood bubbled out of his mouth, staining the carpet black.

Beneath the din of his ringing ears, John heard someone screaming. The noise irritated him. He walked down the hall and saw Crystal cowering in the corner of a cubicle. He put a bullet into her mouth, silencing her and kept going toward the front of the building. Flora, Fauna and Stratus, all stared at him wide-eyed and open-mouthed.   Each got a bullet: Stratus between the eyes; Flora and Fauna between their breasts.

He reloaded his gun in the parking lot, then drove downtown. Three police cars flew past in the opposite direction, sirens wailing. He pulled into an alley, closed his eyes and smiled, happy that Aleister and his friends were finally gone. No more faces, no more torment. He'd beaten them at their game.

He slipped into a peaceful doze, but awoke when someone tapped on his window. Looking up, he gazed into ice blue eyes set deep
in a weatherbeaten face. A greasy baseball cap covered gray hair and a torn ski jacket hung on slight shoulders. A shopping cart filled with old newspapers, a squirt bottle and a squeegee sat beside him. "Wash your windows?"

John stared, dumbfounded, suddenly realizing that the game hadn't ended. He waited for the man's face to change. He knew it would. They always changed. He closed his eyes and heard Aleister's voice.

"Do you want to free yourself from a mindless existence forever?"

John raised the gun and put the barrel in his mouth.

JESSIE

I can hear the beep of the life support and the soft rhythm of its pumps from somewhere behind me. Only a visit from Jessie can make them go away. I hope she comes back like she promised.

She came to see me earlier tonight. If I close my eyes, I can smell her perfume and still feel her warmth from when she snuggled up next to me. Her delicate body seemed made to fit mine; the better half of an incomplete puzzle. Her soft smile, silken blonde hair, and startling blue eyes fill my every conscious thought while the melody of her laughter dances through my mind.

We've shared an infinity of tender moments, yet each one slips away like water through my fingers. Never have I known another human being so capable of stirring feelings from places inside of me I didn't know existed.

"I don't know what I'd do if you left me," she whispered. "You're the only man who means anything to me." The look in her eyes conveyed the message better than words ever could.

"Come on," I teased. "You have guys stashed all over the place. I'm going to get you a big stick to keep the competition

110

away."

She blushed in that sweet way of hers. "They'll be wasting their time You're the only one I want." She threw her arms around my neck and kissed me.

Now that she's gone it's only a matter of time before the nightmares will rush in to fill the vacancy. They get worse every time she leaves. The only thing that keeps me going is the knowledge that she'll be back.

She's always had that effect on me, ever since the first time we met. My buddy Derek threw a party one night. Nothing special. It started out as your typical run-of-the-mill frat party. Joe Satriani on the CD knocking down the walls with his atomic-powered guitar licks, cold beers, and crowded rooms punctuated by clandestine trips out back to smoke pot with Derek.

A comfortable buzz grew in the back of my brain. Derek was going on with a weird story about cannibalism in the mountains when I first saw her. My heart jerked as if someone yanked on a string and the music seemed to stop, then fade like in the movies, only this was real.

She didn't fit in with the crowd who usually hung around Derek. She struck me as being too pure. She had that wholesome fresh-scrubbed look. When her blue eyes caught mine, we connected and my mind cleared as if a fresh breeze had blown into the room. A moment later the music came roaring back full blast. She blushed and turned away. I left Derek in mid-sentence.

"You a friend of Derek's?" I asked when I caught up to her.

"More of a friend of a friend. I've only been in town for a week. My girlfriend Lynn made me come. She thought it

111

would be a good idea for me to get out and meet people." She looked around the room and shook her head. "But I don't think this is my kind of crowd."

"Somehow I knew that. If you're new in town, I'd be more than happy to show you around."

She looked past me as if searching for help. "Well, I, uh... Thank you very much, that's very nice, but I don't even know you."

"Ken." I stuck out my hand. "Ken Reeth. Now you know me."

She looked at me wide-eyed then turned away and giggled. I knew I'd broken the ice. We spent the whole night together, oblivious to the goings on around us. When the party broke up, I went home alone, but I had Lynn's number tucked into my wallet.

It took six phone calls and two dozen roses before she'd go out with me and even then she wouldn't come without Lynn. The three of us went on five or six dates before Jessie would go out with me by herself. She still kids me about it.

My life changed after meeting her — for the better. Nights out with Jessie were movies, plays, and quiet candlelit dinners. Days were reduced to insignificant spaces of my life that got in between the time I spent with her. I kept a steady job. Except for an occasional "night out with the boys," I didn't do much drinking or partying. I'd take a quiet night, snuggled up in front of the television with Jessie anytime.

No, she isn't perfect. She has moments of selfishness and sometimes she pouts if she doesn't get her way, but if things get rough, she's there. The realization of how much she meant to me hit full force when I woke up alone one morning.

"Jessie," I said when I picked her up that night. "I want to be together forever. Marry me."

She hugged me tight. "Oh, Ken. Do you think we're ready?"

"As far as I'm concerned, we don't have a choice. I can't stand being away from you."

"Oh, Ken." Tears welled in those beautiful blue eyes. "I don't know what to say."

"Say yes."

She took my hands in hers and rubbed them on her cheek, then kissed them. "Together forever," she whispered. You mean it?"

"Dammit, Jessie, say yes."

"Yes."

I picked her up and spun her around. "Let's celebrate."

"We'll have dinner and..."

"What?"

"I promised Lynn we would stop by. She's having a get together."

"Tell her we can't make it."

"I promised, Ken. She's counting on us. I can't go back on my word." She folded her arms and I knew she meant business.

"Oh, what the hell. We can at least have dinner alone."

"We'll have dinner, then we'll go to Lynn's."

We celebrated at our favorite Italian restaurant in a romantic atmosphere, good food and superb wine. I felt a warm glow when we left and almost succeeded in talking Jessie out of going to Lynn's in favor of spending the evening alone, but she'd made a promise and wouldn't give in.

As it turned out, we had a great time. When Lynn found

out about our engagement she hugged Jessie, kissed me, and made a big deal out of telling everybody. Drink and conversation flowed easily and the warmth that had begun at the restaurant increased. We ended up staying late and were among the last to leave.

A mile down the road I swerved out of the way of oncoming headlights and flipped over an embankment in a tumble of broken glass, twisted metal, and desperate cries. The last thing I remember is the sound of Jessie's screams. The memory still cuts through my mind like the shard of glass that punctured my lung.

If only I could have done things different. If we hadn't gone to the party. If we'd gone home. If only....

The physical agony of my broken bones and shattered face do not make me suffer enough. The drugs rob me of pain. The anguish of facing what's left of life alone is more than I can bear. The thought of losing her is worse than dying. If Jessie's screams are the aria of an unholy opera, the sadness I feel only adds to the symphony of horror playing nightly in my mind.

Each night she comes to me at the point when it's most unbearable and whispers that she'll never leave me. The tickle of her breath in my ear sends a maddening chill dancing down my spine.

The infernal beeps and maddening rhythm of the life support grow stronger behind me. I long to silence it and the hell that rages through my tortured brain. I'm sure I'm strong enough to crawl out of bed. Strong enough to pull the plug.

Jessie says she'll come back again tonight when everything's quiet. When she does I'm going to do it. I know it's what she wants. I pray that when we're together again, she'll forgive me for getting behind the wheel drunk.

ANIMAL ATTRACTION

Something moved in the bushes.

In one smooth motion, Terry Brunski snapped up his rifle and leveled it in the direction of the sound that came from somewhere outside the circle of orange surrounding his campfire. He paused, his ears straining to hear the noise again.

Nothing.

"Shit." He lowered his gun. "Goddamn scavenger." When he set the gun back in its resting place, he heard another sound, this one off in the distance. "Little bastard can move, too. Either that or he's got friends."

He turned back to the campfire and thought about what daylight would bring. His mouth watered at the thought of fresh venison. *Tomorrow,* he thought gleefully. *Yeah, buddy, come first light I'm going to kill Bambi.* A low chuckle escaped him. *And his mother.*

Terry climbed into his sleeping bag and closed his eyes. The thought of the hunt, especially **THE KILL**, made his whole body hum. An all-too-familiar tingle danced through his groin and he felt himself growing hard. He didn't think he'd be able to fall asleep, but eventually he drifted, his mind flooding with thoughts of **THE KILL**. As he sank deeper into the recesses of his subconscious, his memories retreated to his first experience of tantalizing erotic ecstasy at age nine.

"Look at the cute little bunnies, Terry." His mom pointed to the pen in Uncle Will's back yard. Terry ran to it, leaving his mother behind to talk to Uncle Will.

He stared at the four little puffs of fur nuzzled against their lop-eared mother. The rapid up and down movement of their tiny ribs fascinated him. He reached in and picked one up. It seemed stuck to its mother. He pulled gently and it let go, its teeny pink mouth still moving as he drew it toward him. The mother jumped as if shocked, eyes opened wide.

The heat and the feeling of the bunny's fluttering heartbeat filled Terry with a peculiar warmth. Holding the newborn creature made him feel strong. In control. A sudden urge overwhelmed him and without knowing why, he squeezed. The bunny jerked and twitched, then the heartbeat turned into a warm pulse, as if its pumping contained the strength to push Terry's hand open. Little eyes bugged out of the bunny's head and it squealed, making a sound Terry thought his sister's Barbie doll would make if it screamed. A warm rush shot through him, ending in a delightful tingle in his genitals. His whole world went exquisitely fuzzy.

A moment later, his vision cleared. Blood came out of the bunny's mouth and it went limp. Terry stared at it, then tossed the lifeless body into the pen and went back to the house.

When he grew older, he read that Indians ate the hearts of the animals they hunted in order to take on their spirits. This knowledge convinced him of his special place in nature. He knew that one day, he would kill an animal *and* eat its heart

116

— like an Indian brave. Hunting became a natural hobby. As soon as he learned the necessary skills, he took every opportunity to go off alone into the woods to satiate his hunger.

Hunger.

He opened his eyes to the desolate starlight of the predawn sky and watched the first red-tinged shimmer of the morning sun creeping over the horizon. After a quick cup of coffee, he doused himself with buck lure and set off in search of prey, his metal coffee cup dangling from his belt.

That afternoon he came across an eight-point buck grazing at the edge of a clearing. Raising his rifle, Terry sighted on a spot behind the animal's neck, took a deep breath, let out half and squeezed the trigger. Abruptly, the deer looked up, staring right at him. The rifle jerked against his shoulder, its report shattering the afternoon quiet. The deer froze for a moment before crumpling to the ground. Terry rushed toward it, unsheathing his Bowie knife.

He found the buck twitching on the ground. In a practiced movement, he sank his Bowie knife to the hilt below the rib cage and ripped upward, splitting its ribs up to its neck. The warm blood splashing over his hands made him tremble with anticipation. He yanked the cup from his belt and held it under the steaming blood pumping from the deer's chest. He drank greedily, letting the hot, coppery nectar fill him with a sense of power, then he went to work, deftly gutting the deer, pushing through hot entrails, working his way to its heart.

A moment later, he held the quivering organ in front of him with both hands, staring at it with rapt fascination, wondering how the supplier of lifeblood to another creature could bring him so much pleasure. Before its movement could cease, he thrust the spasming heart into his mouth. With each swallow the blood pulsed into his groin as if it came directly from the buck's heart. Never had he felt so alive. So powerful. So primal.

His erection swelled.

After lugging the carcass back to camp, he prepared a dinner of fresh venison and hot biscuits. Too tired to finish skinning his kill, Terry crawled into his sleeping bag in front of the campfire. He'd finish tomorrow and haul away what was left by noon.

He woke up, thinking he heard noises, but when he sat up, he only heard the crackling from the dying embers of the campfire. He lay back, closed his eyes and listened. Half an hour passed, then he heard them in the bushes as he had the night before. Furtive sounds. Scratchings, scurryings and what sounded like little sucking noises coming from the direction of his kill.

"Fucking scavengers," he muttered.

The noises ceased.

When he heard no other sounds, he rolled over onto his side and went back to sleep.

The next morning, he found most of the buck's hind quarter and flank eaten away. "Shit!" He kicked at the stiff carcass. "Those little..." Then he saw the eye sockets. "Damn. Little rodents ate out the eyes. Bastards burned me. Didn't even leave anything good." He snorted. "It's ruined."

He spent all that day tracking another buck, finally bagging one late in the afternoon. After the orgiastic frenzy of gutting it and drinking its blood, he nearly swooned from the intensity of his pleasure when he devoured the still pulsing heart. By the time he regained his sensibilities the sun had gone down. He dragged the rest of the carcass back to camp, hung it up and scattered parts of it around the site, leaving a trail that led to the body. Satisfied, he snuggled inside his sleeping bag with his rifle and flashlight to wait for his uninvited guests to return. He'd show the little bastards. He checked the action on his rifle. No more free lunches from Terry Brunski. They'd pay for this one. Dearly.

The noises woke him. Slurping, sucking sounds. Tiny footsteps like whispers skittering to and fro. He fumbled for his flashlight and rifle. Light in his left hand, rifle in his right, Terry slowly raised himself onto his elbows and flicked on the flashlight.

It looked as if the buck's hide were a living rug, then his eyes adjusted and he saw that it *was* living. Chipmunks, squirrels, huge rats, weasels, skunks, raccoons, mice and other animals he didn't recognize all fed on the carcass like pups taking milk from their mother. He gasped and two or three of them looked up at him. The biggest weasel glared, its beady eyes glittering in defiance, sharklike teeth dripping, blood red. Terry's stomach did a slow roll.

He raised the rifle and zeroed in on the weasel. The animal kept staring as if daring him to pull the trigger "Fuck you too!"

The shot pierced the darkness, the rifle jumped in his hand, and the weasel splattered backward like a shredded rug. A sound not unlike the cry of a baby followed. Its high-pitched agony drove through Terry's brain like a hot wire. The cry spread to the surrounding woods, echoing through the trees, scattering itself like the animals that rippled out from the remains of the deer.

The rustling of their retreat died like the fading wind, leaving Terry alone to stare at the half-eaten carcass of the buck.

He thought of the bizarre sound the weasel had made and its odd behavior. His skin crept up the back of his neck. "Weird shit. Gives me the Goddamn willies." He chambered another round. "But they're fucking with the wrong dude." He put the safety on, pulled the sleeping bag over his head and listened.

Silence.

When he felt sure nothing more would happen, he allowed himself to fall into an uneasy sleep....

Something brushed his face. He dreamed that a bunch of small furry bodies had crawled into his sleeping bag through some unseen hole.

He jolted awake to a sharp pain in his foot, followed by another on his calf. *My God!* His breath caught in his throat. He opened his eyes and a raccoon lunged at his face, its teeth gashing him below the eye. *Jesus.* A wave of panic shot through him. Terry grabbed for his gun and a pair of needle sharp teeth sank into his fingers.

Screaming, he rolled over to protect himself. Squeals and hisses of protest came from inside his sleeping bag as several smaller animals wriggled out from under him, answering his thrashing with stinging bites to his arms and chest. His breath coming in short gasps, Terry flopped back and forth, feeling little bones crunch beneath his weight. The bites and nibbles persisted, frenzied now. When he pulled his arms away from his face, the raccoons and weasels struck at him, flaying his cheeks and forehead — then an excruciating dagger of pain shot through his scrotum and something burrowed into his groin. He screamed again and somehow managed to climb out of the bag, the animals clinging to his body. He tried to shake them off and bat them away, but they kept coming.

He tried to run, his jerky movements propelling him forward in an insane stagger-dance. He stumbled. Fell. Pulled himself up again. Knife points of pain pierced his muscles. Burning. Burning. Then he felt the hot slash of agony down by his ankle and his Achilles tendon let go with an audible snap, severed by determined teeth. He fell to the ground again and they swarmed, covering his arms and legs.

A fur coat. He laughed in a high-pitched giggle. His body felt like one big gaping wound as he writhed on the ground, arms flailing in a futile effort to keep them from burrowing into his face and neck. His resistance faded as the sheer mass of their numbers weighed him down.

Twin stilettos of white hot agony stabbed into his brain, peaking in a thunderbolt of brightness that flashed through him like a massive short-circuit.

Darkness followed.

He felt something tugging at his eye sockets as if a string had been tied to some anchor point deep inside his forehead. He heard a snap and felt something give, then a liquid warmth washed over and swallowed him. As he faded into the dark wetness, some inner part of him understood. He gave up struggling and realization rushed in with the dimming of his awareness. These animals bore him no malice. They were simply following a higher rule. All they wanted was to take back what belonged to them.

TRICK OR TREAT

I'm wearing my ghost costume tonight. Of course I *always* wear my ghost costume. It's dark and the cold wind's blowing dead leaves around my feet, but I don't notice the cold. What leaves are left on the trees rattle on the branches like whispering monsters. It's really spooky. There's even a full moon. I love Halloween. It's the only time I get to come back to my old neighborhood.

It hasn't changed that much in all this time. My Dad's house hasn't changed at all. It looks broken down and crotchety, just like him. The paint's peeling, the front porch is ready to fall down and his old car with the dent in the trunk is still sitting in the driveway, only now the tires are flat. He doesn't drive it anymore.

I hope this year he'll come with me. I've been coming here every Halloween for the past — don't know how long. Seems like forever but it can't be, I'm only six.

122

Anyway, every year I wait until it's dark and then I go to My Dad's. He never answers the door, but I always see him peeking from behind the curtain. Then I knock.

I don't think he can turn me down much longer. He's getting older. I'm hoping this time he'll go with me, because if it weren't for him I wouldn't be out trick-or-treating in the first place. I'm going to try harder than ever to get him to come out.

I see his house, sitting there looking like I told you it would. The lights are all off like I expected. I can see the curtain moving in the front window. The glow of his cigarette. He's waiting for me.

I hope he comes this time.

I won't run up the steps like I usually do.

This time I'm going to surprise him. There goes the curtain again. He's peeking.

The front door's closed. I'm running along the side of his house, past my rusty bicycle, sneaking up the back stairs. He can't hear me. Through the kitchen door. The hall's dark, but I'm not scared. I know he's in the front room.

I'm at the end of the hall. I see him in the living room. Still looking out the window. For me.

I'm going to jump into the room and surprise him. Loud as I can.

Okay, ready. Deep breath. Go.

"Trick or Treat!"

He jumps. Drops his cigarette. Boy, his mouth looks like he wants to scream, but no sound's coming from it. Now he's grabbing his chest and falling. Twitching.

Oops, wait a minute, he's reaching up and grabbing at the curtain, but it ripped. He's falling down again. Nope, I think he's going to die.

Die.

Hooray, Daddy's finally coming with me.

It's about time.

I've been trick-or-treated like this ever since I can remember, which is — let me see — ever since I was six. The first time he wasn't even giving out candy. He was drunk, like he always is. He was supposed to take me trick-or-treating then, but he had a fight with Mom. She was mad 'cuz he was stinko. I was tired of all the screaming and yelling, and I didn't want to see him hitting her again. When he got really mad, he'd hit me too, so I went outside.

A few minutes later he came out acting like like he was going somewhere. I thought he was finally going to take me trick-or-treating. I came around the corner and walked to the driveway. I heard his car running, but I didn't see anyone in it. I was too small to see over the trunk. Anyway, he backed up real quick and well....

Like I said if it weren't for him, I wouldn't be out here trick or treating in the first place.

JOYRIDE

Leroy leaned back against the wall in the shadows of the underground parking structure and admired the shiny red paint, sleek lines, and chrome of the brand-fucking-spanking new car. The little antenna in the back told him it had a phone. He'd never seen one of these. Didn't even know the make and model which made him want it all the more. He pictured himself behind the wheel calling Janika and letting the bitch know how much class he had tooling around in one of the baddest sleds to ever hit the streets.

He heard footsteps, looked up, and saw an old, geeky looking white dude wearing glasses and carrying a briefcase. The man looked frail in his corny white-bread suit and tie. He came right toward the car. No, couldn't be. This ride had too much class to be wasted on a weak motherfucker like that. Leroy stepped out of the shadows. When the dude's eyes met his, the old man averted his gaze. Fool was scared. Leroy felt his adrenaline kick in.

Sure enough, the man shifted his briefcase to his other hand and went straight to to the driver's door. Leroy's heart pumped faster as he dropped his hand into his pocket and slid his fingers over the cool metal of the .38 he had lucked on in a B and E with his homeboy Reggie. Slipping his finger over the trigger, he wrapped his hand around the gun's butt and hefted it. Its weight felt reassuring.

The old dude glanced over his shoulder, fumbled for his keys, bent down and unlocked the door. Leroy smiled to himself as the emotionless female computer voice calmly announced: "Door ajar. Door ajar. Door ajar."

Leroy moved in smooth like a snake stalking its prey. Gun out —low, next to his hip — he glided forward, easing up behind the old man, trapping him between the open door and the front seat. "Get up off the keys, fool."

The old man gave a little jump before he turned to face Leroy. He clutched the briefcase in front of him as if it would protect him. Old fool looked pasty-faced and weak. His eyes widened behind his Coke bottle glasses when he saw the .38. He had a nervous smile on his face. The computer voice continued its message as if nothing were happening. "Door ajar. Door ajar."

What the fuck was wrong with this cracker? Here he was losing his ride and the motherfucker still smiled. Leroy remembered seeing smiles like that before. Scared smiles. He felt like slapping the man for being so weak. "The keys," he said again.

The dude kept smiling that same stupid, silly-ass grin while he held out the key ring. His hands shook so much, the keys jingled. Leroy snatched them, stepped back, and waved the man aside with the gun. The geek's shit-eating grin started to get on his nerves. On impulse, he gave the old man a quick backhand, sending him staggering sideways. The briefcase flew from his hand and skidded across the lot.

Leroy glared at him while the voice from the car continued in the same feminine monotone. "Door ajar. Door ajar." He hopped into the car and slammed the door, finally shutting up the electronic bitch. He savored the smell of new car leather as the seat belt came down, automatically belting him in, then he jammed the key into the ignition and started the car. The electronic door locks made a solid clunk when he put the car in gear and backed out. He glanced in the rear view mirror as he pulled away. Fool stood there, still smiling — a tiny trickle of blood running out of the corner of his mouth.

"Adios, you gutless motherfucker," Leroy muttered.

He pulled out into the street, turned onto the main drag and headed for the freeway. Shit, that was almost too easy. He braked at a stop light and looked up at the building he had just come from, then at the people passing by. Best get some distance before grandpa called The Man. He reached up to check the visor and saw the geek's picture. I.D. said Jerry Orton, Senior Engineer, Consolidated Robotics. Leroy chuckled. Fool even acted like a robot.

The light turned green. Leroy eased the gas pedal down, enjoying the car's smooth acceleration, leaned back and studied the plush interior, finally zeroing in on the cellular phone. Wait 'til Reggie and Janika see this bad ride. One mean mother fucking sled. He'd do a drive by and show them how much class he had.

He put his hand on the phone, yanking it away when it rang as if it were hot. Say what? A flash of panic rushed through him like the first time he pulled a B and E and the phone rang. Then Reggie's words filled his mind. "What you worried about? Nobody's home. Let the motherfucker ring."

It chirped again.

Maybe it was the geek's old lady. What the fuck, might as well answer, talk dirty to the bitch and let her funky ass quiver at the sound of his voice. He snatched it up.

"Yo, Leroy's Pool Hall, Eight Ball speaking."

"Leroy." The voice sounded flat and conversational like some old grandaddy talking to one of his cronies. "Somehow I knew you'd have a name like that."

"Say what? You talking like you know me. You don't know me from shit, Jack. Who the fuck you think you are? You know who you talking to?"

"Yes, Leroy, I'm quite aware of who I am talking to." The same unruffled tone.

"Is that right."

"That's right."

"Then who the fuck are you?"

"Jerry."

"Jerry? Sound like Jerry-tol. I don't know no motherfucking Jerry."

"Jerry Orton. That's my car you're driving, Leroy."

Smart-ass motherfucker must've had another phone in his briefcase. "Yeah, well it's mine now, so you might as well take your funky ass over to The Man so you can snivel about how some bad-ass named Leroy took it from you."

A fine looking blonde bitch driving a Mercedes pulled up beside him. When Leroy smiled, she looked straight ahead. He hung up, snickering. The phone rang. He let it ring three times before picking it up.

"Give it up, chump."

"You're not being very nice, Leroy." The dude's voice sounded different. Like Leroy's mama used to sound when she was pissed. "You think you can go around being rude, bullying people and doing whatever you want with complete contempt for the law."

Leroy felt a flush of anger. Who the fuck did this cracker think he was? "That's right, Jack. And there ain't a motherfucking thing you can do about it."

"My name is Jerry. Not Jack. And you're wrong, Leroy. Something can be done about it."

"And what's that?"

The seat belt jerked backward, pinning him tightly into the seat. "What the fu..." He dropped the phone, grabbed at the latch and tried to release it, but the mechanism wouldn't budge. He heard a low hum and the electric seat slid smoothly forward, almost pushing him to the steering wheel. He grabbed at the door handle.

It wouldn't move.

He snatched up the phone again. "What the fuck you doing man?"

"Making an example of you."

"Oh, man, come on, I was only messing with you, bro. I'm bringing the car back right now. I was only taking it for a little joy ride."

"I don't want the car back, Leroy. I want my wife back."

"Your wife? I didn't mess with your old lady, man."

"It might as well have been you. You see, one of your — what do you people call them, home boys? Yes, one of your home boys killed my wife and took her car."

Leroy thought he heard a tremor in Jerry's voice. Its tone had gone from cool to cold. So had Leroy's heart. His throat went dry. He started talking fast. "Man it wasn't me. I don't play that shit. I'm just having a little fun. Joyriding, that's all." A steady stream of cars and people passed him, oblivious to what was happening. He thought of screaming for help or maybe shooting out a window, but he felt sure his screams wouldn't be heard. He was almost as sure that the windows would be bulletproof. Even if he did shoot them out, he wouldn't be able to get free of the seatbelt without help.

"How are your hands doing, Leroy?"

The voice jolted him back. "Huh?" The steering wheel grew warm, then hot. He had all he could do to hold on. A few more seconds and he wouldn't be able to touch it. "Chill, man. I can't drive the motherfucker. I'm going to crash!" He held on for a moment longer, dropped the phone and let go of the steering wheel. The car kept going forward. He put his arms in front of his face and jammed on the brakes. The pedal went to the floor.

He didn't crash.

Leroy lowered his hands. Buildings went by, other cars kept passing and the car continued, its steering wheel too hot to touch. At the next corner, the blinker switched on and the car turned right, went another block and turned again. He stared at the steering wheel, looking at it, but not really seeing it.

"Leroy?"

His head jerked up. He looked down at the phone in his lap. "You still with me?"

The phone, Leroy thought. He's controlling it with the phone. He reached down and yanked it out by the cord. For a moment he heard nothing but the smooth hum of the engine, then the lights on the radio flickered and Jerry's voice filled the car in stereo.

"They were quite brutal to my wife," Jerry's voice said. "They couldn't simply take the car. Oh no, they had to do more than that." The seat belt tightened with each word as did Jerry's voice, then the belt started to heat. The blinker switched on again, and the car turned left into a schoolyard. The steering wheel spun hard to the right, throwing Leroy toward the door. He looked out the window and glimpsed two kids staring at him, open-mouthed.

The wheels screeched as the car spun in a continuous circle. Leroy felt light-headed. His stomach rolled. Jerry's stereophonic voice kept talking. "The doctors said she suffered quite a bit before she died. Traumatized. Very uncomfortable." The surrounding scenery blurred. The car went round and round. The seat beneath him felt bumpy, then prickly like a nest of spiders. He struggled to jump up, but the seat belt kept him pinned . "They stabbed her you know." Silence for a moment. Leroy fumbled for the .38. Fuck this shit.

He screamed as bright pain flared through his right thigh and a knitting-needle-sized shaft shot up through his leg. He looked at the blood spattered above him on the car's roof, then at the scenery spinning past him.

"More than once," Jerry's manic-sounding voice said. Another needle shot through his shoulder sending a fine spray of red across the dashboard. His stomach spasmed.

"Quite a few times actually." Another needle sprouted from his left leg. Each jolt of pain made him jump, then he screamed, but a smaller pin through his throat cut it short. He held on to consciousness, fear, rage, and adrenaline rushing through him like windswept litter.

"I'm hoping the others will learn from your fine example."

The radio grew quiet. Leroy sensed only the feeling of spinning, the smell of burning rubber, the screech of tires and his own deep gurgling as the coppery taste of blood gagged him, then the headrest detonated, obliterating his skull. The force of the explosion blew both doors off the hinges.

The car continued circling while its electronic voice dutifully relayed its message:

"Door ajar. Door ajar...."

DYING TO LIVE

2 A.M. Completely still and almost silent, the only hint of sound coming from the soft whisper of liquid nitrogen pumping through the storage banks. Dark, except for the muted red glow of digital readouts blinking in the surrounding blackness like so many eyes. Solitude, the way Norton liked. Peace and quiet. A break from the bitchiness of his never happy wife, Vera.

Norton sighed. Vera. The face of an angel, a model's body, and the warmth of a shark. Norton lived for the moments when she would grant him the privilege of exploring her sensual delights. In her infrequent flashes of passion, he loved her the most, but when the cycle ran its course, she became indifferent, hostile, and finally bitchy.

He went back to the control room, tapped a few keys and watched the information scroll down the screen, checking each of his charges, verifying that the readout on every tank matched the display in front of him. Twelve men and fifteen women, twenty of them head only or "neuros", the other seven "whole bodies." All rested in liquid nitrogen at a cool minus 320 degrees farenheit; the bodies upside down in stainless steel tanks, the heads placed in padded "neurocans" and stored in

133

concrete vaults.

Contrary to his father's predictions, business thrived at Norton's Cryonic Life Extension Facility. Cryonic suspension of a head brought him $35,000, while clients with ample resources could follow the safer route of cryonically suspending their whole bodies for $100,000.

The head-only patients believed their identities would be preserved in their brain and hoped that future technology would make it possible for their other body parts to be replaced through transplantation or regeneration. Though he had his own ideas about how he would resuscitate a person, Norton wasn't so sure you could revive someone after they'd been frozen; but he liked to think of himself as a supplier of hope.

Satisfied with his cross-checks, he leaned back in his chair, propped his feet on the desk and thought of his wife again. A pleasurable tingle passed through his groin. He longed to be with her to feel the curves of her body against his then he remembered the mood she'd been in and the fire in his groin suddenly grew cold.

The way Vera's feelings toward him had.

When they first met at college during his premed days, she'd been sweet and loving. His grades were good, his future bright. He knew when he graduated, his father's money would open doors for him, but when his life became entwined with Vera's, his GPA dropped along with his promising medical career.

When he flunked out of medical school, his dad's influence helped him get a job as a coroner's assistant. Then, with a loan from his father, Norton started the now successful CLEF.

Now Norton, the man who'd married Vivacious Vera, felt lonely, more lonely than he could ever remember. He lived with her, dined with her and had sex with her (when she allowed it), yet try as he might, he could not get close to her.

A sudden beep from the computer pierced the stillness, startling him. The screen flashed a warning message in red.

* NEURO UNIT NINE *
* TEMPERATURE GRADATION ERROR *

Norton's feet hit the floor and his fingers danced across the keyboard, running the computer through its diagnostic loops.

The system checked out.

"Probably a sensor malfunction." He pushed himself away from the desk. Torn between his desire to remain in the solitude of the facility where he paid the price of loneliness and the thought of Vera's companionship at the price of unpleasantness, he grabbed his tool bag and made his way through the corridors between darkened storage banks, until he located Unit Nine. The red LED's flashed minus 320. Steady.

Strange, he thought. The diagnostics check out on the computer end, and the unit seems okay. Probably intermittent. He removed a panel, pulled out his meter, and checked the sensor circuitry. Everything appeared in order.

After replacing the access panel, he sat back and watched the tank, hoping for a change in the readout. Gradually, the susurration of liquid nitrogen lulled him and he dozed.

"Norton," a voice whispered.

He jumped, knocking his tool bag to the floor. His heart pumped wildly. He grabbed his chest and looked around. Red LED's blinked quietly. Liquid nitrogen hissed. Nitrogen!

"Jesus," he said aloud. "Scared the shit out of me. Didn't realize I was so tired. Better go home and get some shut-eye."

He made one last round of the facility, locked up for the

night and drove home.

"Where the hell have you been?" Vera said when he climbed into bed.

He looked longingly at the smooth outline of her figure beneath the covers before he reached toward her. She stiffened at his touch. "Had a problem with one of the units, hon."

She turned away when he kissed her on the cheek.

No alarms woke him while he slept so Norton figured the unit wouldn't give him any trouble, but he checked it first thing the next morning to be safe. It appeared to be functioning normally. He went back to the control room and reran the diagnostics in a continuous loop, hoping they might catch something. Nothing showed.

"Oh, well," he said to the empty room. "Guess I'll wait and see." He stayed in front of the monitor most of the day and well into the night, leaving only to make his rounds. Neuro Nine remained stable. When Norton felt his eyes grow heavy, he decided it was time to go home, but the prospects of dealing with Vera depressed him. No sooner had he completed the thought when the screen flashed red.

* NEURO UNIT NINE *
*TEMPERATURE GRADATION ERROR *

Then in the next instant:

NORTON, DO YOU LOVE?

He did a double-take, but the screen had cleared. He rubbed his eyes and looked again. Nothing.

He ran the computer through a diagnostic cycle, then went and checked on unit nine. Its LED blinked a steady minus 320. He stared at it and for a moment the soft whisper of liquid nitrogen sounded like the voice of a woman. He remembered the voice he thought he'd heard the night before and laughed nervously.

"I'm spending too much time here," he said to the unit.

Norton drove home, determined to spend more time with his wife and try to improve their relationship, but when he stepped inside the house, his only greeting came from the lingering scent of her perfume. He glanced at the clock in the dining room. Two in the morning. Where the hell could she have gone at this hour? He went to the refrigerator, cracked a beer, and sat in his easy chair to wait.

Vera came home twenty minutes later dressed in a short, tight-fitting red silk dress that showed off her shapely legs and ample cleavage. "Look who's here," she said. "Mr. Freeze." Her hair had been piled high in a fancy bun, but now strands of it hung down around her face.

Norton stood, trying to assert his authority. "Where have you been 'til this hour?"

Vera plopped down on the couch across from him and ran a hand slowly up her leg, looked at him and smiled. "Out."

"Where? With who?"

She fumbled for a cigarette, lit it and blew the smoke toward him. "A friend."

He waved the smoke away and felt a flash of anger shoot through his body, ending at his groin. "You're doing this on purpose, aren't you? I know you want a divorce...." He wanted to say more, but the words caught in his throat. She smiled again and ran her tongue across her upper lip. "You're a strange little man who spends all his time with a bunch of frozen stiffs." She paused, her cheeks flushing. "You never have any time for me. There was a time when I could have loved you, Norton.

I wanted to." She threw her hands into the air. "But you're never around. You're nothing but a babysitter for frozen corpses."

Her words provoked both his anger and his desire. He felt himself growing hard. He sat down on the couch next to her. "Vera, honey, let's not act like this. I want things to be right between us." He leaned toward her and kissed her. The smell of liquor and cigarettes assaulted him.

She moaned and drove her tongue into his mouth, reached down between his legs and rubbed him. When he touched the zipper on her dress she pushed him away. "Sorry, hon, but I have a headache."

"What?"

She started to stand up. "You heard me."

Norton pulled her back down to him. "Come on, babe, don't do this to me...."

She slapped him across the face. "Get your hands off me, you pig!"

Hurt and confused, he watched her swaying backside as she strutted out of the room, the sting of her slap still on his face.

Norton woke to the sound of beeping. He opened his eyes and looked around, slowly realizing he had spent the night on a cot in the CLEF control room after fighting with Vera. An empty bottle of Canadian Club lay beside him. When he sat up, his stomach did a slow roll. The insistent beep of the computer pierced his head like a hot wire.

Swinging his legs over the edge of the cot, he stumbled to the console and punched a key to silence the alarm. A red message flashed silently on the screen in front of him.

* NEURO UNIT NINE *
* TEMPERATURE GRADATION ERROR *

He stared at it for a moment, half-expecting something else to show on the screen. When nothing came, he shut off the warning message and started a diagnostic cycle.

Fortified with caffeine and Excedrin, Norton sat in front of the computer and examined the results. Twenty loops and no failures.

"It has to be a sensor malfunction this time." He grabbed his tool bag and followed the corridors to Neuro Nine. The unit awaited him, its display blinking a steady minus 320, liquid nitrogen venting in hushed tones.

"What the hell's going on here?" he muttered.

The steady hiss fluctuated and Norton swore he heard the voice whispering. "Norton. Sweet Norton." Soft and sibilant. "Norton, do you love?"

A trickle of sweat trailed down his spine like an icy finger.

He studied Neuro Nine for over an hour. The temperature remained constant.

So did the sound.

Knowing what he would find, he didn't bother checking on the sensor circuitry. Instead, he followed an impulse and went back to the computer terminal to pull up the "personnel files" of his charges. When he came to Neuro Nine, he accessed the file.

"What a beauty," he sighed when the picture filled the screen.

Green eyes. Emerald green, deep and full of feeling. They seemed to look straight into his heart with compassion and understanding — unlike the hard stares he was used to getting from Vera. Silken blonde hair, high cheekbones, and a heart-shaped face framed those eyes.

His gaze drifted to the information filling the bottom of the screen.

* * * * * * * * * * *

STATISTICS
Name: Marissa Forsythe
Age At Time Of Suspension: 31
Date of Suspension: 11/12/93
Cause Of Death: Auto accident.
* For more information, please access casefile # 420.
* * * * * * * * * * *

He studied her features for a long time before kissing his fingertip and touching it to the screen.

The feelings Marissa's picture stirred made his loneliness more poignant. He decided to go back to the house and make peace with Vera. After all, she'd been drunk. Once sober, she'd be ready to patch things up. He bought a dozen roses on the way home, but when he got there he found Vera gone again. Two half empty glasses sat on the coffee table alongside an overflowing ashtray. Marlboro butts mingled with lipstick-stained Virginia Slims.

Hot tears came to his eyes. His hands shook. His stomach tightened as if an icy fist had punched him. He couldn't bear the thought of Vera with another man. He stormed out the door and tossed the roses in the gutter.

For hours he drove aimlessly, finally ending up back at the CLEF control room in front of a blinking computer screen. Not bothering with the diagnostic, he went straight to Neuro Nine to find the steady blink of its readout and the familiar murmur of liquid nitrogen.

"I don't know what I'm going to do," he said to the hollow room. His sobs echoed off the walls. "I've worked hard, provided for her, loved her. I've done everything I knew to make her happy."

He blinked away his tears aware that the steady rhythm of the LED faltered. The sound of escaping nitrogen whispered softly. "Norton, do you love?"

"Yes, I love," he said, not caring whether or not the voice were real. "I love so much, it hurts. How can she do this to me?"

"I love, Norton," the voice whispered again. A cold breath tickled his ear, sending an icy caress dancing down his spine. "I want to be loved." A little louder this time. He realized that it was a female voice, no longer outside him, but *in* his mind. Frightened, he put his hands over his ears and shut his eyes.

"Don't be afraid," she continued, her tones soothing and comforting.

Norton thought of the green eyes he'd seen earlier and the feelings they'd stirred. "Marissa?" His voice shook.

"If only I'd had a chance. I could have loved you."

Norton couldn't believe this was happening. Part of him wanted to bolt from the room, the rest of him felt irresistibly attracted. "No one else can hear you, can they?

"Only you, my love."

"Jesus, I'm losing it."

"I'll stop if it bothers you."

Norton thought for a moment. The sound of her words in his head had scared him at first, but he feared loneliness more. And her voice didn't *sound* bad. Her words felt as if they belonged — and they matched those lovely green eyes. "No," he said haltingly. "Please don't stop. I — I..."

"What?"

"I know how crazt this sounds, but so is talking to someone who's dead." A nervous titter escaped his lips. "I've looked at your picture. Studied your file. And I think — I think —" Then the words gushed forth. "I love you."

"Oh, Norton." Her voice choked with emotion. "I love you too."

"But how?"

"You've been so loving and attentive, taking care of me for all these years. I've come to know you and feel what you feel. Every time you've been sad, I've been sad. I know what your wife has been putting you through. I've felt it too. It breaks my heart to see you hurt. I've tried so hard and so long to reach you, but now I think I've made a mistake."

"What do you mean?"

"Now that we've made contact, it's even more painful. Oh, Norton. I want so much to — to...."

"To what, Marissa?"

"To *touch* you, Norton. *Feel* your warmth. Your love." She started to cry and he found himself crying with her, two sets of emotions spiraling through his brain, each feeding off the other until he felt as if his brain would explode. He ran from the room holding his head.

When his emotions subsided, he longed to go back, but couldn't bring himself to return to the sadness of her voice. He fell asleep in front of his terminal, Marissa's angelic countenance watching over him in the darkness from the soft glow of the computer screen.

When he woke and saw her gazing at him from the monitor, he thought his experience had been a dream. Eagerly he went back to Neuro Nine, relieved when Marissa greeted him. He found her an understanding and sympathetic listener, something Vera never had been. Norton didn't go home that night.

Over the next few days, the line dividing day and night blurred. He spent most of his waking moments talking with Marissa and as time passed, his love for her grew deeper. When he wasn't engrossed in conversation, he gazed longingly at the image of her face on his monitor, often falling asleep in front of it. In one sense he had never felt more complete, but the impenetrable barrier that separated him and his true love proved to be a source of unending frustration as did his growing sense of inevitability. He would eventually have to face the cold, harsh reality awaiting him at home in the form of Vera.

It hit him hard one evening when he awoke from a nap, realizing he needed a change of clothes.

"I'm sorry, Marissa," he said to the storage tank, "but I've got to go home and talk to her."

"I understand, my love," she said.

Norton could hear the hurt in her voice. "Believe me, if I thought I could change things I would. I'd divorce her, but she'd take me to the cleaners. Besides, it wouldn't help us any. If I thought it would, I'd say to hell with the money."

"I know. No matter what happens, I'm here for you. I'll always love you, even if we're forever separated."

When Norton spotted the strange car parked in front of his

house and flickering candlelight in the bedroom window, his rage kindled. He drove to the end of the block, parked at the corner and walked back to the house. Taking his shoes off at the end of the driveway, he stole around back and slipped in the kitchen door. Inside, he heard the sound of a man grunting, Vera's passionate moans (with more fervor than he'd ever heard), and the rhythmic creaking of bedsprings. His heart pounded wildly in his chest and his temples. His throat tightened. His fingers clenched into fists.

"Bitch!" he muttered. Tiptoeing down the hall, he stopped at the closet and groped in the darkness. "Bitch!" he whispered as his sweaty hands found his baseball bat. He crept down the hall, stopping outside the bedroom door.

Vera's moans came quicker as did the grunts of her partner. Norton peered into the candlelit room and saw his wife's legs spread wide on the bed, her partner's bare back moving up and down between them. "Bitch!" he said between clenched teeth.

A sharp intake of breath cut through the room and all activity ceased.

The man's head popped up and Norton swung the bat. It caught the side of Vera's lover's head ting with a sickening thud that reminded Norton of the time he ran over the neighbor's dog. The nude body of Vera's lover went sprawling over the side of the bed like a limp duffel bag.

Vera screamed and huddled against the headboard as Norton turned toward her. Her eyes darted from the bat, to Norton, to the limp body of her lover. White shards of bone glinted in the orange glow of the candlelight. Black fluid oozed from the crushed side of his head.

"Go ahead, you spineless little twerp," she said. Her voice

sounded high and tight. Her eyes had widened until Norton could see the whites around the irises.

He froze.

"You piss-poor excuse for a man. You don't have what it takes to satisfy the needs of a *real* woman."

Norton stared uncomprehending.

"Mr. Freeze with his little popsicle dick!"

He started toward his wife with the bat raised.

Vera fainted.

"Cold," Vera said between chattering teeth. Her lips had turned blue. Gooseflesh covered her nude body, now submerged in an ice bath. Straps held her arms and legs immobile. Norton checked the temperature. 38 degrees.

Perfect.

"It'll be over soon." He turned away from her.

"What'll be over soon?" she cried. "Enough is enough, Norton...."

"I think we're ready now." He turned back, syringe in hand.

"What do you think you're doing?" Her voice quavered.

"Something to relax you, that's all."

Vera opened her mouth to protest and Norton plunged the needle into her arm. Whatever words she'd intended died in her throat.

With asbestos gloves, he released the seal on the Neurocan holding Marissa's head, opened the lid and submerged the whole unit in a silicone oil bath which raised its temperature from the -320 of liquid nitrogen to the relative warmth of -110. When the temperature stabilized he removed her from the silicone and lovingly placed her in a tray on a cart. The thin film of oil covering her skin and hair made her smooth features look baby soft and angelic.

After securing hoses to the main arteries of her head, he flicked the "ON" switch. The rhythmic cadence of the heart-lung
machine filled the CLEF's operating room. Beside it stood the CPR machine. Yellowish glycerol pumped through the hoses to Marissa's head, raising its temperature even more. Norton checked the gauge on the unit, then went to work on Vera.

When the temperature of Marissa's head matched that of Vera's body, Norton pumped the head dry and repositioned the heart-lung machine. Moving quickly, he severed Vera's head and replaced it with Marissa's, catching the blood beneath the neck wound in a tray and recycling it through the heart-lung machine. The actual switch took him only a few seconds. He had a minor problem aligning the jugular veins, but the rest went smoothly. He verified Marissa's pulse then took her out of the ice bath and wrapped her in a blanket. Vera's head went into the empty neurocan and back into Neuro Nine.

Exhausted, Norton retrieved the cot from the control room and set it up next to Marissa. Then he took her cold hand in his and fell asleep.

"Norton?"

He heard her voice whispering in his mind and felt cold fingers moving in his hand. He thought for sure he was dreaming.

"Norton, my love, I can see you!"

His eyes flickered open and gazed into Marissa's. His heart swelled with joy. "Marissa!"

"I can see you, Norton. But I feel weak. I can't move my neck. It hurts. I'm cold."

He sat up and kissed her tenderly on her pale cheek, unconsciously flinching at the icy texture. "It's all right, darling. You need rest and time to recover. Let me give you something to help you sleep and relieve the pain."

She smiled weakly, then he gave her a shot of sedative, wrapped her tightly in the blanket and took her home where he crawled into bed with her. He fell asleep trying to warm her with his own body heat.

"Make love to me," she said softly. "I want to feel your warmth in me."

Though her skin still felt clammy, Norton thought she felt warmer than before. He realized with embarrassment that he was becoming aroused. He pulled her closer and spoke softly. "You're still weak, love. Maybe we'd better wait."

"I can't wait. I need you to hold me, love me."

Norton gave in to his rising passion and pressed his warm lips to hers, his tongue hungrily exploring the recesses of her mouth. Then he made love to her gently, tempering his excitement with tenderness.

They made love often as the days passed, but Marissa remained weak and had to stay in bed. At first Norton thought her skin felt cold and hard, but now that time had passed, he could tell it had definitely softened. He went to the CLEF only when necessary and performed his duties quickly, always hurrying back home to Marissa who waited for him in bed. Norton doted on her, constantly bringing flowers and gifts, spending long hours snuggled up to her, telling her of his plans for the two of them.

He didn't know when he first became aware of the smell, only that it permeated everything. A cheesy smell. He tried to ignore it, but as the days grew warmer the odor intensified.

One morning he awoke to the sound of knocking. He didn't want to get up to answer the door, so he waited for his unwanted visitors to go away. He heard a crash a few minutes later, then footsteps and voices. "What a stink! Over here. The bedroom."

Norton sat up and the door to his bedroom flew open. Two uniformed policemen burst in. Wide eyes took in the room, then the men retreated retching. "My God! He's in bed with a ripe one."

A moment later a man in a suit stepped in with a handkerchief over his mouth. He flashed a gold badge. "Mr. Morris, you're under arrest for the murder of your wife and her lover."

Murder?

Norton wondered what had gone wrong. How could they have found out?

Vera's laughter filled his mind.

He leaned over and kissed Marissa gently on the lips. "Don't be afraid, love," he whispered. "Vera can't prove a thing."